LONELY

D0532502

He calls himself 'Melody' — the word burned inside his belt. Because he can't remember his own name — or anything at all prior to the past six weeks. It's 'amnesia', according to Regan Avery, the woman he rescues from a fast-flowing river. But Melody doesn't need the fancy name for his predicament to know he's in trouble — for the few things he *can* remember involve being shot at and wounded, with a posse hard on his heels . . .

STEVE HAYES

---◆---

LONELY RIDER

Complete and Unabridged

LINFORD
Leicester

First published in Great Britain in 2015

First Linford Edition
published 2017

A catalogue record for this book is available
from the British Library.

ISBN 978–1–4448–3114–6

Published by
F. A. Thorpe (Publishing)
Anstey, Leicestershire

Set by Words & Graphics Ltd.
Anstey, Leicestershire
Printed and bound in Great Britain by
T. J. International Ltd., Padstow, Cornwall

This book is printed on acid-free paper

This is for you, Tom

1

After his long parched ride across the hot desert scrubland, the river winding through the canyon below him looked inviting.

Reining up at the edge of the bluff overlooking the canyon, he sat there in the saddle looking down at the cool, swift-moving water for several minutes — until finally his horse, equally thirsty, pawed impatiently at the ground with its foreleg.

'Okay, okay,' the man grumbled. 'Don't bust a gut. We'll be down there soon enough.' Gently removing his wounded left arm from inside his shirt, he tried to straighten it. It was stiff and when he forcibly straightened it out, pain shot down from his bicep into his forearm, making him wince. He slowly rolled back the bloodied shirt sleeve and examined the gash in the soft tissue of his triceps. It was now protected by a scab of dried blood, which indicated it was healing. Luckily, the bullet fired three days ago by one of the posse members had only nicked the outer flesh and not caused any injury to the muscles. But it had hampered the man at a time when he needed his health and his wits in order to keep eluding the lawmen pursuing him, and he knew that until it healed he had to be extra careful in order not to get captured.

It was an intimidating thought. What made it worse was he had no idea what crime he'd committed or why he was a hunted fugitive; he just knew that if he didn't want to be caught and jailed or worse, perhaps strung up, he had to keep running.

Wearily slipping his arm back inside his shirt, which served as a makeshift sling, he wiped away the sweat that was running down his face and nudged the tired, long-legged, copper-colored bay down the steep winding trail that led to the river.

It was another twenty minutes before they reached the canyon floor and rode out of the oak trees growing alongside the bank. At once, rider and horse felt the temperature drop as cool breezes blew in off the churning rapids. Downstream, in the direction of the Mexican border, the falls sounded like distant thunder. For some reason that eluded the man, the river, the rapids and the falls all seemed strangely familiar. He wondered if he had grown up around here and if so, hoped that he'd finally find someone who would recognize him and tell him who he was. Not knowing why he was being hunted was bad enough; not remembering anything about his past made him feel like the loneliest man on earth.

Ahead, between the rocks and bushes bordering the riverbank was a footpath. Dismounting, the man led the bay to the water's edge. There he let go of the reins so the horse could drink. It did so, greedily, while the man knelt beside it, removed his hat and dunked his head into the shallows.

The water was icy cold and he stayed under until his ears ached. Then straightening up, he shook his head like a wet mongrel and leaned back on his heels. He remained this way, warily looking about him, until he felt refreshed enough to gently dip his wounded arm into the water. Instantly, blood from the shirt sleeve and his wound turned the water pink. But on the plus side, the icy water numbed his arm and for the first time since he'd been shot two days ago, he was free of pain.

Beside him the bay was still drinking.

'Damn fool,' the man cursed. 'You want to bloat up?' Rising, he grabbed the bridle with his good hand and pulled the horse's head out of the water. The bay resisted and took a nip at him. But the man had grown accustomed to its responses during the past few weeks and jumped back avoiding its teeth. 'Go ahead,' he told it. 'Act like a crazy stinkbug. It'd serve you right if I let you drink all you can and then watched your belly swell up till it hurt so bad you couldn't walk.'

The horse ignored him. It was not ill-tempered, merely stubborn, and it stood still while the man dunked his canteen in the water, waited until the bubbling stopped showing it was full, then withdrew it, screwed on the cap and hung the strap over the saddle horn. Then gripping the saddle horn with his good hand, he stepped up into the saddle. As he did the bay suddenly reared up. For once the man wasn't expecting it and had to grab hold of the long flowing black mane so he wouldn't be thrown off.

But instead of being angry, he gave a slight chuckle and said: 'Happy now?'

The horse snorted, satisfied by its display of defiance, then turned and started away from the river.

That was when the man heard the cry of distress.

2

It came from the direction of the rapids.

Whirling the horse around, he stood up in the stirrups and looked upstream. But he couldn't see anyone in the water, merely the fast-moving whitecaps racing past him. Wondering if he'd imagined hearing the panicked scream, the man gave one last look at the rapids. Then, still not seeing anyone, he was about to nudge the horse forward when he heard a second cry for help.

This time he knew he hadn't imagined it. Squinting in the bright sunlight, he scanned the river in both directions. Again, he saw no one. But as he checked upstream for a second time, he glimpsed a bare arm thrashing above the whitecaps and a moment later, the face of a terrified young woman bobbing in the rapids.

Her head disappeared almost immediately as she was dragged under by the current. But by then the man had leapt from the saddle, grabbed his rope and was one-handedly unlooping it as he waded out into the water. He stopped when he was waist-deep and in danger of being swept off his feet by the undertow and again scanned the river for signs of the woman.

When he next caught a glimpse of her she was twenty feet upstream from him. He yelled at her as loudly as he could, his voice barely heard above the rushing water, and started twirling the noose above his head. He knew he'd only have one shot at her before she was swept past him and over the falls, but years of roping steers and wild mustangs running at full speed served him well. He gave a final confident twirl and then flicked his wrist, sending the noose spinning out toward the woman.

She still hadn't seen or heard him, and was shocked when the noose settled over her arms and torso.

The man braced himself as the rope snapped tight, the weight of the woman combined with the force of the current almost jerking him off his feet. But he somehow remained upright and ignoring the pain in his wounded arm used it and his other arm to quickly pull her toward him. The river wasn't about to surrender its victim so easily though. Despite pulling with all his strength, the man felt himself losing the battle as he was slowly dragged deeper into the water.

Turning, he whistled and at once the bay obediently trotted into the water toward him. When the horse was close enough, the man wrapped his end of the rope around the saddle horn and yelled at the bay to back up.

The horse obeyed, retreating until it was on dry land. The man grabbed the taut rope and pulled himself ashore. There, he was able to drag the half-drowned woman to the water's edge. Though young and strong-limbed, she was too exhausted to crawl onto the bank. The man kneeled beside her. He hesitated, at first uneasy about touching her. Then necessity overcame his shyness and slipping his arm under her, he lifted her from the water . . .

3

Eyes closed, she lay on her back on the grass, her long wet straggly hair wrapped around her face, her arms and legs so still that if her breasts hadn't been heaving as she desperately fought for breath the man wouldn't have known she was alive.

He waited for a few moments, then knelt beside her and cradled her head on his lap. Changing positions made her cough so violently, she almost choked. Then without warning she rolled onto her side and began vomiting. When she was finished, she coughed a few more times then turned over and sat up. On seeing the man, she recoiled fearfully and started to scramble away from him.

Not wanting to add to her fear, he didn't follow her but stood up, almost as tall and straight as the trees behind him, his voice gently reassuring as he said: 'No need to be afraid, ma'am. I don't mean you no harm.'

She sat there, huddled against the rocks, shivering, eyeing him suspiciously, not sure if she should believe him. But frightened as she was, she saw honesty in his wide-set gray-green eyes and sensing there was something trustworthy about this man, made no attempt to run.

Slowly, so as not to alarm her, he drew his Colt and tossed it onto the grass in front of her. She looked at him for a moment as if in a daze; then she picked up the gun and held it with both hands, one finger on the trigger as she pointed it at the man.

'I know how to use this,' she warned hoarsely. 'Don't think I don't. What's more, I *will* shoot you if you come any closer.'

The man sighed, irked that his attempt to set the woman at ease had failed. Hunkering down on his heels, he plucked a blade of grass from the ground and calmly chewed on it as he studied her.

His stare unnerved the woman. 'Are you one of them?' she demanded.

'One of who?'

'Those men . . . the bandits that robbed the stage I was on?'

'Do I look like one of them?'

'I'm not sure. They all wore masks — kerchiefs tied around their faces.'

'How 'bout the rest of me? Were any of the men my size or dressed like me?'

'I don't know. I was so frightened I got down on the floor and hid, and . . . '

'Look,' he said when she didn't finish, 'I don't blame you for being scared, ma'am. Being robbed is enough to make anyone's blood run cold.'

She didn't say anything. But some of the fear left her pretty, farm-fresh face.

'But ask yourself this . . . if I *was* one of them, why would I give you my gun?'

Unable to think of a suitable answer, she remained quiet.

'And why would I go to the trouble of saving you when you might recognize me as one of the robbers? Especially since — as you can see — I've been shot myself. I mean, with all due respect, ma'am, that just don't make a hill of sense.'

She couldn't argue with that. 'No,' she agreed after a long pause, 'you're right, it doesn't.' She lowered the gun, the last of her fear vanishing from her red-rimmed cobalt-blue eyes. 'I'm sorry, mister. You just saved my life and here I am, accusing you of being a bandit. I should be ashamed of myself.' She tried to get up but she was too weak and her legs collapsed under her. The man hurried to her side, gently lifted her up and held her steady until she was able to stand on her own.

'Thank you.'

'*Por nada.*'

'Will you please forgive me?' she asked, offering him her hand.

'Reckon it'd be rude not to,' he said, shaking hands. 'Miss . . . ?'

'Avery . . . Regan Avery. And you are?'

He hesitated.

Misunderstanding his silence, she said: 'Look, you don't have to tell me who you are if you don't want to. I know that some people out here are reluctant to tell strangers their nam — '

'It ain't that, Miss Avery,' he interrupted. 'I'd be happy to give you my name — *if* I knew what it was.'

Regan frowned, both puzzled and curious. 'You don't know your own name?'

He shook his head.

'How can that be?'

He shrugged. 'Truth is, ma'am, I don't know nothing 'bout myself. 'Least not past six weeks ago. Anything beyond that, my mind's a complete blank.'

'How fascinating,' Regan said. 'I've never met anyone who had amnesia.'

'Had what?'

'Amnesia. Loss of memory.'

'Am-neesh-ur?' he stumbled over the

word. 'Hm-mm. Never heard it called that afore.'

'I'm not surprised. It's a relatively new term, coined from Classical Greek: amnesia, meaning forgetfulness.'

'Reckon I don't feel so dumb when you put it that way.'

'You shouldn't feel dumb at all. I only recently came across the word myself while I was studying medicine in New York. I was in the library and saw it in a book written by the French psychologist, Theodule-Armand Ribot. It was called, *Les Maladies de la memoire*, which translated means Diseases of Memory. It wasn't part of my studies, but once I started reading it, I found the subject of amnesia absolutely fascinating and couldn't put it down.'

'Well, I don't mean to contradict you, ma'am, or say you ain't smart, but fascinating ain't what I'd call it. Not knowing who you are or where you're from is more like pure torture.'

'I'm sorry,' Regan said quickly.

'Please forgive me for being so insensitive. Of course, it must be simply horrible. It's just that — well, like I said, I've never known anyone with amnesia before.'

'No need to apologize, ma'am. I'd probably be curious myself in your shoes.' He paused as he considered what to say next and then, as if thinking aloud, said: 'Melody.'

'I beg your pardon?'

'It's a word burned on the inside of my belt. I don't know if it's me or the name of the person who owned the belt afore me — or even if it's a name at all. But it's what I've been calling myself when folks asked me my name.'

'Melody? . . . Melody?' Regan cocked her head and listened to how it sounded. 'Well, it's a nice enough name but — '

' — not fit for a man,' he finished ruefully. 'Yeah, that's what I figured. But since it's the only name I got, *and* the only link to my past, I'm kind of stuck with it.'

'There's no need to apologize,' Regan said. 'Truth is, Mr. Melody, I rather like it. It's pleasant to the ear and unusual. On top of that . . . ' She paused and studied him, water still dripping from her wet butter-colored hair and then added: ' . . . it suits you.'

'It does? Why?'

'Because *you're* unusual. You're so tall and . . . so polite and . . . and seem so, well, trustworthy.'

'How can you know that? We just met.'

'That's exactly my point. Even though I don't know you, Mr. Melody, and you've recently been shot by God knows who, I trust you. Don't ask me why. I just do. And I don't trust many people, which makes you — unusual.'

'Well,' he admitted, 'I suppose it ain't so bad to be trustworthy . . . or unusual.'

'In your case, it's a compliment. Compared to most of the young men I met back in New York, you're as different as chalk and cheese.'

He frowned, not sure if that was good or bad.

'I know it's a silly expression,' Regan said, laughing. 'Yet I use it all the time. Must be something Freudian, don't you think?' She laughed again. It was infectious and though Melody had no idea what Freudian meant, he laughed along with her.

It felt good to laugh. It was the first time he'd laughed in six weeks, when he'd awakened in the desert with no idea who he was or where he was or how he'd gotten there . . . and looking around saw the bay standing patiently nearby . . . reins dangling as if it had thrown him off but hadn't run away. He realized, of course, there was a chance that the horse wasn't his at all. It could've belonged to anyone. He wouldn't know. Not in his present condition. Hell, for all he knew he might have killed its owner and stolen the horse. He hoped not because even without a memory, he instinctively thought horse thieves should be hung on the spot. But he had to admit it was certainly possible. All he knew for sure was that the horse had been standing beside him when he regained consciousness.

Regan's voice interrupted his thoughts. ' . . . that's what I'll call you from now on.'

'Chalk and cheese?'

'N-N-No,' she laughed. 'Mr. Unusual.'

'Reckon I've been called worse.'

'Haven't we all,' Regan said, adding: 'I wonder, would you do me a favor? I don't live too far from here. Just a few miles west of the bridge and — '

'What bridge?'

'Seven Mile Bridge. It's upriver a ways. You didn't see it?'

Melody shook his head.

'I'm surprised. It's been there forever — 'least, long before Silverton was founded.'

Melody shrugged. 'Reckon I must've ridden in from another direction.'

'Must have,' Regan said, adding:

'That's where the robbery took place. The bandits must've known the stage crosses there because they were waiting for us behind the rocks on this side.'

'Anybody hurt or killed?'

'Uh-uh. Though I was lucky you were around or I probably would've drowned.'

'What did you do that made them throw you in the river?'

'They didn't throw me in. I jumped.'

'Why?' he said, surprised. 'Surely no jewelry's worth risking your life for?'

'Jewelry wasn't what was on their mind, Mr. Melody. I jumped because they tried to rip my clothes off. That's when I decided any fate was better than what they intended to do to me.'

Melody nodded, understanding.

'Anyway,' Regan added, 'I know it's a lot to ask, especially when you've just saved my life — '

'You want me to take you home, that it?'

'Would you?'

'I reckon . . . '

'Thanks. And in return, when we get there I'll bathe and bandage your wound so it doesn't get infected. I'll also fix you something to eat. Well, at least Annabelle — our cook — will. You just tell her what you want and she'll make it for you.'

'You can't cook?'

'Of course I can. In fact I'm a great — No,' she said, interrupting herself, 'that's a lie and I can't lie to someone who just saved my life. The truth is, Mr. Melody, I'm utterly hopeless when it comes to cooking. I'm sure that sounds strange to you, living out here, where women spend half their lives in the kitchen, but you see, I never had any reason to learn. We've had a cook and servants for as long as I can ... Oh God,' she exclaimed. 'Will you listen to me? I sound like such a spoiled brat.'

Melody let that pass.

'I'm really not, you know. It's just that I haven't been near a kitchen since father announced he was sending me back east to boarding school. I didn't want to go, but I had no choice. So as a going away present, I baked Daddy a berry pie and of course it turned out to be a disaster. That was six — no, seven years ago. I've been studying medicine in New York ever since I left college, but then three weeks ago I decided to come home and hang out my shingle here. I'll have to take the local exam, but I'm sure I can pass it.' She paused and sensing that Melody was tired of listening to her, said: 'I didn't mean to bore you. I was just trying to explain why I can't cook. But Annabelle's a wonderful cook. She'll fix you a great home-cooked meal.'

Relieved that she'd finally stopped chattering, he nodded.

'Good. It's a deal then.' She offered him her hand and he shook it gingerly, as if afraid it might break.

4

He couldn't remember the last time he'd felt the touch of a woman. But because it felt so strange, so unfamiliar, he guessed it must have been a long time. Nevertheless, he had no trouble liking it. Against the calluses formed by years of roping, her skin felt as soft and velvety as a filly's muzzle. But to his surprise there was more to it than that. Holding her hand hadn't just been pleasurable. It had also made him feel less lonely, less alone, and it was with great reluctance that he let go.

'Reckon we ought to get started, ma'am. That's if you're up to it?'

'Yes. I'm fine now, thanks.'

He led her to his horse, stepped up into the saddle, reached down and pulled her up behind him.

'Hang on tight,' he warned as they rode upriver, away from the rapids.

'This pony tricks you into thinking he's got manners and then, when he figures you ain't paying attention, he acts up and next thing you know, you're on the ground seeing stars.'

'Sounds sneaky.'

'Sneakier than a two-bit crossroader dealing base.'

'Dealing what?'

'From the bottom of the deck.'

'Oh . . . I've never heard it called that. And what's a crossroader?'

'Card shark.'

'Ah-huh. How interesting.' She paused as an idea struck her, then said: 'What other ways do card sharks cheat, do you know?'

'Sure,' Melody said without hesitation. 'Some fellas use slight-of-hand tricks to swap unwanted cards with ones up their sleeves, while others put a blister on certain cards — '

'Blister?'

'A tiny bump so the cheater can feel it and know what card it is when it's facedown.'

'Oh-h . . . '

'Why do you ask?' he said, curious. 'You interested in gambling?'

'Me? Good heavens, no.' She laughed, amused by the idea. 'It merely crossed my mind that you might have been one.'

Melody held up his good hand. 'With these calluses? No chance. Gamblers' hands are as smooth as a woman's cheek and their fingernails are always well-groomed.'

'Really? Why's that?'

'So they can feel any nicks or cuts they mark the cards with — ' He stopped as he heard himself and then exclaimed: 'Sweet Jesus, maybe you're right, ma'am. Maybe I quit cowboying and took up poker for a living?'

'Or the other way around?'

Melody nodded, mind churning but producing no satisfactory answers.

'Does that sound logical?' Regan asked. 'Like something you might do?'

'No. I hate gamblers.'

'Why?'

'They're short on integrity, long on cheating.'

'If you can't recall anything, how do you know that?'

He frowned and silently asked himself the same question. 'I don't know,' he admitted. 'Maybe just instinct.'

'Think harder,' she pressed. 'Try to remember. The reason must be buried in your brain somewhere.'

'If it is, it's staying hidden. Reckon it's just a feeling I got. But you're right, ma'am. How else would I know 'bout gamblers unless I used to be one?'

'It would make sense,' said Regan. 'But for now I wouldn't worry about it. It was just a hunch. Until we have proof, I wouldn't put too much stock in it, Mr. Melody.'

'You'd be doing me a favor, if you'd drop the mister and just call me Melody?'

'Only if you call me Regan?'

'Fair enough.'

'There's something else I want you to

do. I want you to think about gamblers and gambling and then tell me if it brings any other thoughts or images to mind.'

He thought, trying to visualize himself as a poker player or even a faro dealer, but each time he ran into a blank wall.

'Nope. Sorry.'

'Ah, well, no matter,' she said, disappointed. 'It probably doesn't mean anything. And if it does, I'm sure you'll eventually remember it.'

They rode on through the dense, bushy undergrowth and flowering Palo Verde trees in silence. The roar of the rapids and the falls gradually faded behind them.

'What about your saddle?' Regan asked suddenly.

'What about it?'

'How did you come by it?'

'I don't know. Bought it, I guess. Why?'

'I was wondering if maybe you won it in a poker game. You know? From someone who couldn't cover his losses?'

'Anything's possible, I reckon.'

'What about your horse?'

'What about him?'

'Where'd you buy him?'

'Beats me. Truth is, ma'am, I don't know if I did buy him. Or even if he is mine, for that matter. He was just standing there when I come around.'

Regan nodded, mind racing, and then asked: 'What's his name?'

'No idea,' Melody said.

'Then what do you call him?'

'Names I can't repeat in front of you.'

Amused, Regan laughed and shook her head. 'A wounded man with amnesia called Unusual Melody who might be a gambler and has a no-name horse. My goodness, I'm really going to have fun trying to explain you to my father.'

5

After leaving the Rio San Carlos — which Regan told Melody was a tributary of the much larger Gila River — they rode southwest for another two miles across sunbaked scrubland that stretched all the way to the distant Pinaleno Mountains. Towering over the range was Mt. Graham, a sacred peak known by the Western Apaches as *Dzil Nchaa Si An* or Big Seat Mountain. Closer, and to the west, was a range of low sun-scorched hills that were no more than a mile away.

The landscape didn't look familiar to Melody. He didn't get any sense of having been there before either, as he had at the river. Disappointed, he shrugged it off, as he'd done many times over the past weeks when he'd ridden through towns or stopped at various ranches to water his horse and no one recognized him. Occasionally he glanced back to see if there was any sign of the posse. Each time there wasn't he felt more secure and less concerned about his injury, which was recovering fast.

Behind him, Regan sensed Melody's disappointment. She clasped her arms around his waist even tighter as if she were trying to assure him that eventually everything would be all right, and said cheerfully: 'It's not much farther. Just beyond those hills.'

'Your father's spread, you mean?'

'Spread?'

'Ranch.'

'*Ranch*?' She laughed as if he'd tickled her. 'Good heavens, no! My father doesn't own a ranch.'

'He don't?'

'No. And it's lucky for him he doesn't. Poor Daddy wouldn't have the vaguest idea of how to run one. Why, I doubt if he's ever been on a horse in his life or even knows the difference between a stallion and a gelding. Not unless someone pointed it out to him or he had to make a ruling in court.' She gave another bubbling laugh before adding: 'I'm sorry if I said anything that led you to that conclusion.'

'You didn't. I just figured, living 'round here he'd either be a rancher or a miner.'

'He's neither,' she said. 'Daddy's now a bank manager.'

'Now?'

'Before that he was a Circuit Court judge.'

Melody looked impressed. 'Your pa was a *judge*?'

Regan nodded. 'He retired while I was still in New York. Said at his age, all the traveling was too exhausting.'

'A circuit judge?' Melody repeated. 'I'll be damned.'

Curious, Regan asked: 'Does that mean something to you?'

'I don't know.' He thought, long and hard, then shrugged. 'Maybe. I ain't sure.'

'Think again,' she insisted. 'Try to

picture a judge and a courtroom and see what other images come to mind.'

He closed his eyes and tried to think of any reason that might lead him back along the chains of his memory, brief as it was, linking him to a judge or the law.

'Nope,' he said eventually. 'Mind's still a blank.'

'That's too bad. For a moment there I thought we'd hit on something.'

They rode on in silence, each occupied by their own thoughts.

Ahead, the sun-scorched hills were now less than a half-mile away. The two nearest hills sloped down together, forming a natural V-shaped hollow. Though the town buildings and roof-tops didn't show in the hollow, the tall white spire of a church did.

Melody stared at it, wondering if Silverton had any connection to his past. Though nothing came to mind, he felt strangely uneasy — as if he were about to stick his head into a hangman's noose.

'Maybe I killed someone,' he said

abruptly. 'Maybe I was in court being sentenced and got shot when I somehow escaped?'

'Nonsense!' Regan said. 'You're no more a killer than I am. I'd bet my life on it.'

'I hope you're right,' Melody said gloomily. 'I can't think of anything worse than being locked up for the rest of my life. Hell, I'd sooner be hanged!'

6

As they rode out of the sun-bleached hills and followed the winding trail leading to Silverton, Melody grew more and more uneasy. Wondering why, and if his uneasiness was related to a crime he'd committed there, he asked Regan to tell him everything she knew about the town.

Frankly, she replied, she didn't know very much. But from what she'd heard from her father and various family friends Silverton had been founded in 1852 and owed its existence to the many rich silver mines in the sur-rounding hills. She added that once every month large deposits of the precious ore were brought into town by heavily-guarded mule-trains and locked overnight in the bank vault. Then the next morning at exactly 10:07, the bullion was escorted by more armed guards to the station to await the arrival of the 'Silver Train,' as it was nicknamed. When it did arrive, always at exactly 10:21, the bullion was loaded into a car equipped with a safe that had a time-lock, and then shipped to the U.S. Mint in Denver.

The whole operation ran with the efficiency of a Swiss watch. No one could remember the train ever being late or the bullion delivery being off-schedule. More importantly, in the six years that her father had been manager, there had been only one attempt to rob the bank and that turned out to be a failure, with all but one of the robbers being killed or captured. Compared to the numerous bank and train robberies that occurred in other towns throughout the Southwest that record was a minor miracle and the folks of Silverton were justifiably proud.

'My father was responsible for most of that efficiency,' Regan continued as they reached the outskirts of town.

'When he took over as manager of the bank neither the train nor the bullion deliveries were on time. The miners just showed up when they showed up and loaded the bullion onto whatever train arrived next. As a result there were lots of robberies. Daddy changed all that. He set up a strict schedule and made sure everyone adhered to it.' Guessing Melody might not know what adhered meant, she added: 'In other words, he insisted they follow his orders to the letter.'

Melody whistled softly. 'Bank manager *and* Circuit Court judge — your pa, he doesn't lose much speed when he changes horses, does he?'

'No,' Regan agreed. 'And before he was a circuit judge he was Vice President of the Atherton Mining Company.'

'They control most of the silver mining 'round here,' Melody said, impressed. 'Why did he quit that job?'

'I'm not really sure,' Regan said. 'That was when I was a baby and from what I gather, Daddy had a falling out with the Directors and either quit or was fired — it depends on who's telling the story.'

'I doubt if he was fired,' Melody said. 'Not if he went on to be a bank manager.'

'It doesn't seem likely, does it?' Regan agreed. 'The funny thing is, though, Daddy had to be coaxed into accepting the bank position. When he retired from the judiciary system, his goal was to spend the rest of his days catching up on his reading and, if he felt really energetic, falling asleep beside a fishing hole.'

'What changed his mind?'

'That's a good question, Mr. Melody — '

'Melody, remember?'

'Melody . . . ' Regan thought a moment before continuing. 'I kept asking him the same thing and he always ducked my question. Then, one day he finally stopped sidestepping me and said that he'd promised my mother, right before cancer took her, to always make sure I had the best of everything. He added that he'd put away some money but he was worried that it might not be enough to see me through school and support me once I was on my own, so decided to accept the bank position.'

'So it was you and wages that swayed him?'

'You could say that. But in all fairness, the incentive bonus was more than wages. Only a fool would have turned it down and my father's no fool; especially when it comes to money. Though he never told me exactly how much the bonus came to, it was enough to buy our home, pay for my schooling and, according to Daddy, put sufficient money into a trust fund so that I'll never have any financial worries.'

Melody pursed his lips in a silent, appreciative whistle.

'Once that problem was taken off his shoulders,' Regan continued, 'Daddy's whole demeanor changed for the better. He stopped being moody and grumpy and became fun to be with again. At least, until lately.'

'Lately?'

'Yes. Recently, he's gone back to being grouchy and gets upset at the least thing.'

'Probably all that new responsibility. It can wear down even the best of men.'

'Yes, I suppose so. It wouldn't be so bad, you know, if he'd only tell me what's troubling him. Then maybe I could help. But he keeps it all bottled up and I'm afraid that one day it will all be too much for him and he'll have a stroke or a heart attack.'

Melody tried to think of something to say that would lessen her anguish. But, as usual, the words he wanted to say refused to surface and he remained silent.

'I do know one thing that bothers him,' Regan continued. 'Daddy's determined that neither the Silver Train nor the bank will ever be robbed while he's manager. He's made it his top priority. He even hired Pinkerton agents, not just to guard the bank but the silver shipments as well. Some of the Directors were against it at first, claiming it was too costly. But after time passed and there weren't any hold-ups in town or up in the hills where the mines are, they changed their minds and praised Daddy for it.' She paused as Melody chuckled, then asked: 'What's so funny?'

'I was just thinking,' he said wryly. 'I hope I ain't that one bank robber who got away or else you're going to have even more of a problem explaining me to your pa.'

'There's no fear of that,' Regan said, laughing. 'The bandits were all wearing masks. So no one would be able to recognize you — even if you *were* that robber.'

Melody didn't say anything, but inwardly he felt a sense of relief and wondered why.

7

The Merchants Bank of Arizona was on the corner of Front and 2nd Streets. A large, bleak, brick-and-stucco building with barred windows, it was the largest bank in the territory. Two Pinkerton agents guarded the front door, two more patrolled the lobby and banking area and another two were never far from the heavy steel doors that prevented intruders from reaching the massive vault. It was not an eye-pleasing building, but it was considered to be the safest bank in the whole Southwest.

As Melody and Regan rode along Front Street toward the bank, several passersby recognized her. Most of them smiled or waved, but at the same time they gave Melody puzzled looks.

'They're wondering who you are and how you got shot,' Regan said. 'They're also wondering why I'm riding behind you. They probably don't think it's proper of me, the daughter of the manager of their precious bank to have her arms wrapped around a stranger.' She giggled wickedly. 'Actually, they should thank me — 'specially the old ladies. I've given them something to gossip about for weeks to come.'

'It's a good thing they don't know 'bout my amnesia,' Melody said, 'or you'd have the whole town lined up to see if they can figure out who I am.'

'Yes, and with my luck,' Regan joked, 'someone like Miss McDermott, Queen of the Old Maids, will swear you're John Wesley Hardin or Billy the Kid.'

They had reached the bank. Melody reined up, dismounted and helped Regan down.

'Maybe I should wait here while you go talk to your pa,' he suggested.

'What on earth for?'

Melody didn't answer. He stood there in the broiling sun, uneasily biting his lip.

It took Regan a few moments to understand why. Then, 'I don't believe it,' she said. 'You really are worried that you might be a fugitive or a murderer, aren't you?'

Melody shrugged. 'It ain't impossible, you know. Hell, I can't think of a logical reason why I was lying unconscious in the desert. And I doubt if you can either.'

'Nonsense! I can give you plenty of logical reasons. Your horse stepped in a gopher hole or was startled by a rattler and threw you, or you passed out because of the heat — which plenty of people out here do by the way — things like that, none of which suggest you're wanted for murder. Please, Melody,' she pleaded, 'stop being so negative and trust me. I'm a very good judge of character.'

His silence was noncommittal.

'I'm serious,' she continued. 'You have to stop worrying. Believe me, when you do get your memory back, you'll probably laugh at how ordinary

the reason is for why you were there.'
Before he could reply, she stepped close, stood on tiptoe and pecked him on his sweaty, stubbly cheek. 'Now, come on,' she said, grasping his uninjured arm. 'Let's go inside and have a nice cool glass of lemonade and I'll introduce my father to the man who saved his daughter's life.'

8

Theodore Avery sat in his office at the bank, drumming his large meaty fingers on his desk, desperately trying not to think the worst. But though he was generally an optimistic man, who always tried to find the positive side to even the bleakest of moments, today he was hard-pressed to be anything but negative.

The stage from Phoenix was two hours overdue and he couldn't make himself believe the excuse that clerk at the stagecoach office had given him: that either a wheel had come loose or an axle had broken and the driver and the guard were having trouble fixing it. Instead, Avery had a gut feeling his daughter was in danger and there wasn't a damned thing he could do about it, except wait and hope that he was wrong.

The minutes dragged by and still no sign of the stagecoach. Almost beside himself with worry, Avery glanced at the wall clock for what must have been the hundredth time and realized only a few seconds had passed since the last time he'd looked.

Suddenly, it got too much for him. Jumping up, he told his secretary that he would be gone for the rest of the afternoon. Shocked, because he believed in everyone working until the last second of their shift, she asked him where he was going — 'You know, sir, just in case someone like the mayor happens by and asks where you are?'

'To see what happened to that infernal stage!' he yelled and stormed out.

His loud voice attracted the attention of everyone in the bank, customers and employees alike. As one, they turned and watched as he stomped to the front door and jerked it open — only to collide with someone coming in.

Avery started to apologize then

stopped as he saw that the person he'd almost knocked down was his daughter. He was so surprised, he couldn't say anything but just stared at her, mouth open, wordless for one of the few times in his life.

'D-Daddy!' Regan exclaimed. 'Where on earth are you going in such a hurry?'

'I — uh — uhm — '

'What is it you keep telling me?' she teased. 'Regan, sweetheart, always take your time, never rush into anything and always, always look where you're going.'

'I — I'm sorry,' he said. 'I wasn't expecting — I mean, the stage is two hours late.'

'That's because we were held up.'

'H-Held up?'

'Yes, by four men. Just this side of the bridge.'

'Oh-my-God, was anyone hurt?'

'Uh-uh.'

'Well, that's a relief.' Avery paused and then as a thought struck him, looked uneasy. 'Tell me something. Did you happen to get a look at — I mean did you or any of the other passengers see who the robbers were?'

'No. They all wore kerchiefs over their faces.'

'Oh-h ... ' He sounded more relieved than disappointed, and had to force himself to add: 'Dammit, that's too bad.'

'I've been trying to remember what the one man's voice sounded like, but — '

'What one man?'

'The one who spoke — who told the guard to throw down the strongbox. I think he was the leader, but I was so frightened I — '

Her father quickly pressed his finger over her lips, silencing her. 'Of course you were, sweetheart. Who wouldn't be?'

'But — '

'No, no, you stop worrying your pretty head and — ' He broke off as if suddenly seeing her for the first time. 'Your hair, Regan? It's all — '

'Wet. Yes, I know. So, obviously, are

my clothes. That's because I jumped into the river.'

'The river?'

'Yes, to get away from the bandits. Look,' she added before her father could interrupt, 'I'll explain everything later, Daddy. The main thing is, I'm fine and so are all the other passengers.'

'Thank heaven for that!' Avery expelled all his concerns in a loud sigh and then hugged his daughter. 'And you say the bandits, they took the strong box?'

''Fraid so. But what's money compared to human lives — nothing, right?'

'No, no, of course,' he agreed without conviction. 'But the river? My God, sweetheart, you might have drowned.'

'I probably would have, but for Mr. Melody here. He saved my life — literally.'

'Mr. Melody,' Avery said sincerely, 'I'm indebted to you beyond words.'

'Anyone would've done the same thing,' Melody replied. 'I just happened to be there at the right time else I

49

wouldn't have been able to snag her with my rope.'

'But you *did* snag her, young fella. That's all that matters. My daughter means the world to me and, frankly, without her around I doubt if life would be worth living.'

Regan, sensing how uncomfortable her father's praise was making Melody, said: 'I've promised to bandage his arm and — '

'How did you get shot, young fella?' Avery interrupted.

'It's a long story and we'll tell you all about it later,' Regan said before Melody could answer. 'Meanwhile, we're both hungry, Daddy. So if it's all right with you, I'll take him home now and have Annabelle fix him something.'

'Of course, of course — though a meal, home-cooked or not, seems like a poor reward for saving your life.'

'What else do you suggest?' Regan said.

Her father ignored her and turning to Melody, said: 'I'll never be able to repay you, son, but I promise you this: from now on I'm going to spend every waking moment trying to figure out ways I can!'

Melody again shifted uncomfortably.

Regan, before her father could continue, grasped Melody's hand, saying, 'Bye, Daddy,' and dragged him out of the bank.

Outside, in the late-afternoon sun, she let go of Melody's hand, saying: 'Don't mind my father. He's a bit overbearing and his enthusiasm can get on your nerves, but he means well. He really does. And behind all that blustering is a sincere and genuinely honorable man. What's more, like him or not, he means every word he says.'

Melody nodded as if understanding, but there was a glint in his eyes that suggested he wasn't completely sold on her father.

'So unless you want to pass up your chance of having the best home-cooked meal in all of Arizona,' Regan teased, 'not to mention my 'charming' company, you'll take me home.'

Melody studied her, long and hard, thinking that without a doubt she was the most gabby woman he'd ever known — and though he couldn't remember how many woman he knew, he sensed it was more than a few. But at the same time she was one of the prettiest and definitely one of the nicest, and since he needed a safe haven to hole up in while he tried to remember who he was, he allowed himself a slight smile and said: 'Be my pleasure, ma'am.'

'Wonderful. And who knows, Melody. Maybe your longing for a home-cooked meal is just your mind's way of pointing you toward your past.'

'Let's hope so.'

'And even if it isn't,' Regan said, 'at least when you leave you'll be stuffed full of good food.'

9

As they started to walk toward Melody's horse Regan abruptly stopped and stared at two riders that were dismounting in front of Yardley's Mercantile across the street.

'What's wrong?' Melody asked her.

'Those men,' she whispered. 'I think — no, I'm sure they're two of the bandits who held up the stage.'

Melody sized up the two hard cases. Small, scrawny gunmen in their thirties, their clothes were caked with dust and their hats were pulled down low over their bearded faces. Each carried two six-guns in low-slung, tied-down holsters and had a Winchester tucked in the saddle scabbard.

'What makes you think so?' Melody asked quietly.

'One of the robbers had a red bandanna over his face — like the one the short man has around his neck — and I recognize that buckskin belonging to the other man.'

'You're sure 'bout that?'

'Pretty sure.'

'I need you to be more than 'pretty' sure.'

'Very well . . . ' Regan looked at the men again and nodded. 'It's them. I'm sure.'

Satisfied, Melody unhooked the tiny safety strap holding his Colt in his holster and spoke out the corner of his mouth. 'I wasn't suggesting you were wrong. It just seems mighty peculiar that they'd be in town right after robbing the stage.'

'I agree. But it's definitely them. I know it is. Also, look at their saddle-bags. See how full they are? I bet they're stuffed with money.'

Melody saw the bulging saddlebags and nodded, convinced. 'Okay. Now listen carefully and do exactly as I tell you.'

'W-Why? What're you going to do?'

'Never mind. Just move away from me. Go on,' he insisted when she didn't move. 'Start walking . . . slow and easy . . . so as not to attract their attention.'

He waited for her to obey him then stepped into the sunbaked street and walked toward the two gunmen. Their backs were to him as they tied their horses to the hitch-rail. And by the time they turned around so that they were facing him, Melody was halfway across the street.

Their reaction surprised him. By their expressions it was obvious that both bandits not only recognized him but were afraid of him and their hands immediately dropped to their six-guns. They continued to watch him and as Melody got closer, his purposeful stride and the grim look in his narrowed gray-green eyes warned them that he was coming for them.

Both went for their guns.

They were alarmingly fast but Melody was faster. And deadly accurate.

Each gunman staggered backward as

a bullet punched a hole in his chest. Both stood there for a heartbeat, eyes wide with shock . . . then they dropped their guns and crumpled to the ground.

Melody holstered his Colt almost as quickly as he'd drawn it.

Everyone on the street had stopped at the sound of gunfire. Now as Melody approached the dead gunmen, people came hurrying over and milled around him.

'Stand back, stand back!' a voice of authority ordered. 'Dammit, let me through!'

The crowd obediently pulled back so that a small gray-haired man with a drooping, salt-and-pepper mustache and a town marshal's badge pinned to his shirt could pass through.

'You!' he barked at Melody. 'Is this your doing?' He indicated the corpses and at the same time kept his shotgun trained on him.

Melody looked down at the diminutive lawman and nodded.

'Okay. Then keep your hands where I

can see 'em, mister.'

'Tom, stop it!'

Marshal Tom Garrett turned as Regan came hurrying up.

'Mr. Melody's a friend of mine, Tom. He had no choice but to shoot these men.'

'Care to tell me why, Miss Avery?'

'They were reaching for their guns.'

'You sure?'

'Enough to testify to it.'

'I see . . . ' Garrett lowered his shotgun and turned to Melody. 'You got some kind of quarrel with these fellas?'

'Nope.

'Ever seen 'em before?'

'Not that I can remember,' Melody said truthfully.

'He went over there on account of me,' Regan said. 'I told him they were two of the men who robbed the stage I was on and — '

'Whoa,' Garrett stopped her by raising his hand. 'You sure of that, Miss Avery?'

'Yes.'

'How 'bout you?' Garrett said to Melody. 'Were you on the stage too, mister?'

Before Melody could reply, Avery broke through the crowd and joined them. 'Tom, Tom,' he said condescendingly, 'save your questions for later, all right? Can't you see my daughter's shaken up?'

'Mr. Avery, I'm sorry but — '

'Tom,' Avery said sharply, 'I'm telling you to leave her alone!'

The marshal stiffened as if slapped. There was an awkward pause as the crowd looked on, waiting to see what the little lawman would do next.

'Listen, Tom,' Avery said, his tone softening, 'I don't mean to step on your toes or tell you how to do your job. My only concern right now is for my daughter. So how about if I give you my word that I'll bring her — and Mr. Melody here — to your office later? By then everyone will have calmed down and you can question both of them all you want. Fair enough?'

The marshal knew there was no point in arguing with Theodore Avery, one of the best-liked and most important citizens in town, so with a resigned shrug he lowered his shotgun.

'Very well, Mr. Avery. But I'll expect to see the three of you within the hour.'

'You can count on it, Tom.' Avery turned to Regan: 'You all right, sweetheart?'

'Yes, yes, I'm fine, thank you, Daddy. But you're right about feeling shaken up.'

'It's no wonder. Good Lord, who wouldn't be?' He gave her a fond hug and then turned to Melody. 'Reckon I'm even more indebted to you now, young fella.'

Melody shrugged in a way that could have meant anything.

'Daddy,' Regan broke in, 'I think the money from the strongbox is in the bandits' saddlebags.'

'Really?' Her father didn't sound as

pleased as she expected. 'I hope you're right. Tom,' he told the marshal, 'take a look, will you?'

Garrett nodded and went to the nearest horse. Opening one of the saddlebags, he stuck his hand inside and pulled out a fistful of silver dollars.

'I'll be damned! If that don't that beat all.'

His words were drowned out by a rousing cheer from the crowd.

Avery forced himself to smile at them. 'This is our lucky day, folks!'

Again, everyone cheered.

'Tom,' Avery said to the marshal, 'while I look after my daughter, will you turn over all the money to the bank, please?'

It was an unnecessary, condescending remark and the marshal sounded offended as he said: 'Sure, Mr. Avery. Right away, sir.'

'C'mon, you two,' Avery told Regan and Melody. 'I think we can all use a drink. At least I know I can.' He led them toward the Lucky Dollar, a saloon near the bank.

'All right, all right,' Marshal Garrett barked at the crowd, 'show's over, everyone. Get moving!'

10

Inside the Lucky Dollar, everyone was discussing the gunfight. They broke off as Melody, Regan and her father entered and quickly crowded around them. Some of the men sized up Melody while the others eagerly questioned Regan about the shooting.

Her father quickly shut them down. 'All right, boys, that's enough! My little girl's had all the excitement she can handle for now.'

'Can you at least tell us who those gunmen were?' one man asked Regan.

Before she could answer, her father said: 'Mr. Melody, here, had no choice but to shoot them, if that's what you're wondering, boys. If he hadn't, they would've gunned him down like a dog in the street. I saw it all happen from the bank window.'

Giving no one a chance to ask any

more questions, he ushered Regan and Melody to a nearby table. There, as they got seated, he gave Melody an inquisitive look.

'You're plenty fast with that iron, young fella. Plenty fast.'

Melody ignored him.

'I've seen a lot of gunfighters in my time, son, so I know what I'm talking about.'

'Daddy, please — '

'Men with reputations stretching clear to Texas and back. Hell's fire, I've seen 'em all — Sam Bass, John Wesley Hardin, Luke Short, Ben Thompson, you name 'em, I've seen 'em. And by God, I have to say, you slap leather with the best of 'em — '

'Daddy,' Regan insisted, 'I said that's enough! We came in here for a drink, remember?'

'Of course, of course,' agreed her father. 'A drink! You're right, sweetheart. Yes, well, let's order then. Harley,' he said to the bartender. 'Three whiskies, if you please. And make sure you pour them from your good stock. None of that Coffin Varnish you palm off on drummers or scab herders passing through.'

'Sure thing, Mr. Avery. Coming right up.' The bartender took a bottle from under the bar, poured three whiskeys, brought them and the bottle to the table and quickly returned behind the bar.

Avery raised his glass in toast.

'To you, young fella,' he said to Melody. 'Silverton's man of the hour!'

Melody inwardly cringed. But he managed a curt nod and the three of them drank. The whiskey went down smooth and comforting, and he poured himself another.

'I've been trying to think how I can repay you,' Avery continued.

'Father, I'm sure Melody doesn't want — '

'There's a lot of good land for the taking 'round these parts. If I were to invest in a parcel of it — maybe buy up one of the ranches that's about to go into foreclosure, for instance — would you consider being my foreman and running the whole kit and caboodle for me?'

'Daddy!'

'Hush now for a sec, little girl,' Avery told Regan, 'let me hear what Mr. Melody thinks of my offer.'

Melody fought down his irritation and said coldly: 'Thanks, but I've never run a spread or wanted to. You'd be better off hiring a man with more know-how.'

'Normally, I'd agree with you,' Avery said. 'But, you see, son, this wouldn't be ordinary ranch work. This would be part of a wedding present I plan on giving my daughter when she finds a young man she's partial to — '

'Father,' Regan said angrily, 'will you stop talking as if I'm not here? You're embarrassing me.'

Avery ignored her and kept his gaze locked on Melody. 'Would that be something you might find more appeal-ing, young fella?'

Melody bit back his disgust for Avery. A dangerous little smile creased his tight-set lips but never reached his gray-green eyes.

'Don't reckon it would,' he said. Then to Regan: 'No offense meant, but until I can remember who I am and where I'm from, it wouldn't be fair to ask any woman to be my partner.'

'I heartily agree,' Regan said, still fuming. 'Anyway, I'm closer to spitting blood than I am to getting hitched. Now,' she added, rising, 'if you two will excuse me, I got things to do.' She stormed off, the batwing doors swinging shut behind her before Melody and her father had time to politely get to their feet.

'Dammit to high heaven,' Avery said admiringly. 'I sure love that little girl. She's got so much fire and grit I swear there are times when I can't tell her from her dear departed mother!'

He waited for Melody to say something. When he didn't, Avery drained his glass, stood up and offered

Melody a big meaty hand.

'Don't leave town right away, young fella. I'll figure out some way of showing my gratitude. I may be an old goat who talks too much, but I got more aces up my sleeve than a riverboat gambler.' He hurried after his daughter, leaving Melody sitting there, with the same crooked little smile creasing his tight white lips.

11

Now that the shooting was over and the undertaker had loaded the bodies of the dead gunmen onto the mortuary wagon, everyone in the bank returned to work.

Everyone but Avery, that is. He stood at the window, watching as Regan and Melody walked to his horse. He sighed heavily, obviously distressed about something, and entered his office. There, he sat at his desk, idly sorting through paperwork as if everything was normal. But though he tried to appear at ease, there was an underlying concern creasing his expression that indicated he had troubles gnawing at him.

Outside, Regan and Melody paused beside his horse. Untying the reins he mounted, reached down and pulled Regan up behind him and together they rode off.

It was only a short ride to the Hinkley Mansion, which sat like a forbidding sentinel at the edge of town. Behind it the sun-scorched desert scrubland stretched for innumerable miles until finally it reached the brown foothills of the Pinal Mountains. It seemed impossible to think that any form of life could exist in such inhospitable terrain, yet high above a nearby canyon, silhouetted against the bright, eye-achingly blue sky, a handful of buzzards circled over a dying coyote; while in the distance a Red-tailed hawk drifted on the thermals, in search of its next meal.

Melody reined up at the large brick mansion, dismounted and helped Regan down.

'Well,' she said, smiling, 'what do you think of home sweet home?'

Melody arched his dark eyebrows in what amounted to a noncommittal shrug.

Regan laughed and shook her head at him.

'What?' he said.

'You,' she said.

'Me, what?'

'Mr. Unusual.'

Melody frowned. 'Meaning?'

'Your reaction. I should've known you'd be the only person who wasn't impressed by it.'

He looked at the mansion again to make sure he hadn't missed anything. He hadn't.

'It's big,' he allowed.

'Careful,' Regan teased, 'you're making my heart race.'

Melody gave a rare smile that vanished almost as soon as it appeared.

'Truthfully,' she pressed, 'don't you think it's magnificent?'

'Mountains are magnificent.'

'You're comparing this house to a mountain?'

'No. Seems like you are, though.'

Regan gave an exasperated sigh. 'Dear God,' she breathed. 'If you aren't the most frustrating man alive I don't know who is!'

Melody looked surprised. 'I don't mean to be.'

'Don't apologize. It's why I like you.'

''Cause I'm frustrating?'

'No. Unusual, remember?' When he didn't respond, she added: 'Well, let's not stand out here in the sun. Come inside and I'll have Annabelle fix that meal for you.' Melody's expression didn't change, yet inwardly he seemed to retreat.

'Another time, maybe.'

'Why? What's wrong?' she said, surprised. 'Lose your appetite?'

'Reckon . . .' He pulled his eyes away from hers and toed the ground with his boot.

'Well, you should still let me fix that arm. If it gets infected — '

'Thanks, but it'll be okay . . . ' He paused, as usual unable to fully express himself in the presence of a woman.

Regan, stung by his rejection, shrugged. 'Very well . . . suit yourself.'

They stood there in the sun, the

silence between them growing awkward.

'Well, I have to go,' Regan said suddenly. She hurried to the front door, opened it without a key and went inside. The big oaken door slammed thunderously behind her.

Angry at himself, Melody stood there another moment and then turned to his horse. 'Next time my tongue is tied in knots, you might want to kick me.'

The bay snorted and tossed its head, flecks of foam spraying everywhere.

Melody one-handedly swung up into the saddle and sat there, reins in hand, staring at the mansion. He didn't know why but he felt drawn to it. Wondering if it had anything to do with his past, he was about to ride away when he noticed a raggedly-dressed barefoot boy watching him from nearby. A towhead, with freckles bridging his pug nose and skin burned brown as tobacco, there was an independent maturity about him that made him seem older than his ten years.

Melody immediately felt at ease around him.

'It's haunted, you know,' the boy said.

'The house?'

'Yup.'

'You sure 'bout that?'

'Don't have to believe me, mister, you can ask anyone. They'll tell you.'

Melody, hoping to pry some useful information about both the mansion and Avery from the boy, played along. 'This ghost — you ever see it?'

'Lots of times.'

'What's it look like?'

'Give me a dollar and I'll tell you.'

Admiring the boy's gall, Melody dug out a handful of silver, found a ten-centavo coin and flipped it to him.

'This won't buy you much, mister.'

'You'll get another ten if I like your story.'

'And if you don't?'

'You can kiss the backside of my horse.'

The boy made a face, but pocketed the coin.

'The ghost, it looks just like Mr. Hinkley. Only you can see through him. And he floats 'stead of walking.'

''Be damned.' Melody hid a smile and probed deeper. 'This Hinkley fella? He a relative of Mr. Avery?'

'Yeah. Some kind of great uncle. He died soon after Mr. Avery come to Silverton. If he hadn't, he'd still be living here.'

'How do you know that?'

'Cause Gramps says that's what Mr. Hinkley told him back in '56, when he built the place. Said he planned on dying in it.'

'So your grandfather knew Mr. Hinkley?'

''Course. They was cousins. 'Cept they never talked to each other.'

'Why not?' Melody said, curious.

'On 'count of Mr. Hinkley cheating Gramps out of his share of the mines they found.' The boy stuck his hand out for more money, but Melody ignored it.

'So Mr. Hinkley's fortune came from mining?'

The boy nodded. ''Cept he didn't just find one mine, he found *two*. One right after another. Or so he says. Grampa swears *he* found the second mine. He just didn't stake a claim to it right off and when he finally got 'round to going to the claims office, Mr. Hinkley had already registered it in his name.'

'Claim-jumping your own cousin — that's 'bout as low as it gets.'

'That's what Gramps said. Made him so angry, he tried to kill Mr. Hinkley. Shot him twice and would've gone on shooting him 'cept the marshal stopped him.' The boy paused before sadly adding: 'Gramps is still in prison on 'count of it.'

'And Mr. Hinkley, he lived?'

'Sure. Dug enough silver ore out of them mines to make hisself the richest man 'tween here and 'Frisco. Didn't do him no good, though. Right after that he got religion and the wheels came off the wagon.'

''Meaning?'

'Mr. Hinkley got religion. Said God came to him while he was sitting in the outhouse, reading the Good Book. Told him that he'd been put him on earth to save the wicked. No one believed Mr. Hinkley, but he didn't care. First thing he done, he took up with a whore and learned her how to read and write so she could be a school marm. Then he married another sinner, a painted dancehall girl from Tucson, who told him to buy all the saloons in town so he could save the souls of the other sinners working in 'em. And then,' the boy said darkly, 'Mr. Hinkley, he decided to save all the folks in Silverton, so he stopped selling whiskey and served buttermilk instead.'

Melody couldn't help but chuckle.

'It's true, mister. I wouldn't lie 'bout something as awful as that.'

'I believe you,' Melody said. 'Finish your story.'

'It's finished. Soon as Mr. Hinkley tried to make everybody drink milk, his luck went sour.'

'Mean he went broke?'

'Worse than that. He lost a leg when his wagon overturned, then he got bit by a Gila monster and the poison turned him blind. After that his wife got sick and died. And finally he went soft in the head and hung himself in her bedroom. 'Least that's what Mr. Avery claims and he's the one who found him. 'Course, no one believes him. Mr. Hinkley, he could barely walk and couldn't see nothing, so how's he going to be able to climb up on a chair and hang himself.'

Melody had to admit the boy made sense. 'Why would Mr. Avery want to hang his uncle?'

'To get all his money, 'course, him being the only relative and all. Most folks say that's why Mr. Hinkley haunts the place. Say he's trying to find a way to avenge hisself on Mr. Avery.' The boy held out his hand again.

Melody, amused by the boy's imaginative spiel, tossed him another ten centavos. The boy caught the coin, bit it to make sure it was real and then pocketed it.

'One last thing,' Melody said. 'How long has Mr. Avery lived here?'

'He and his daughter moved in right after Mr. Hinkley went blind. Mr. Avery, he said he owed it to his uncle to look after him till he died. 'Course no one believed him. They all knew it was his way of tricking Mr. Hinkley into signing the house and all his money over to him.' The boy paused and held out his hand for another ten centavos.

Melody ignored him. Giving the mansion a final look, he turned the bay around and rode back into town.

From her upstairs bedroom window Regan watched Melody riding away. She was still smarting from his rejection. But when she turned from the window and saw her reflection in the wall-mirror, the wholesomely pretty face that stared back at her gave her enough confidence to hope that Melody would be back for her sooner or later.

12

At that same moment, her father sat looking out the open door of his office, nervously watching as Marshal Garrett entered the bank. Nodding respectfully to the Pinkerton guards, the veteran lawman went to one of the windows. There, he gave the teller a handful of silver dollars and a deposit slip, and waited patiently as the starch-collared, mustachioed young man handled the transaction.

Hot as it already was in Avery's office, the sight of the marshal seemed to make it even hotter for him and taking out an expensive silk monogrammed kerchief, he mopped the sweat from his florid brow. Pull yourself together, he admonished himself. No one suspects you. And even if they did, they can't prove a damn thing.

Knowing that should have made him

feel better. But it didn't. And as Avery watched the marshal, he envied his calm, unruffled demeanor.

Finished with his business, Garrett turned as if to leave — then stopped as he caught Avery's eye and waved cheerfully. Avery half-heartedly waved back and the marshal, accepting that as an invitation, approached and entered the office.

'Afternoon, Theo,' he said, closing the door. 'Sure it is a hot'n, ain't it?'

Avery nodded and cleared his throat in an effort to get rid of his nervousness. But nothing changed and lowering his voice, he hissed: 'What in Sam hell happened out there at the bridge?'

'Easy, easy,' Garrett said affably. 'Nothing to lose your teeth over.'

'Your men kill a Pinkerton agent riding shotgun and you want me to take it *easy*?'

Garrett shrugged callously. 'Ain't like getting worked up will bring him back to life.'

Avery took a deep breath to control himself. 'You swore nothing could go wrong, damn you! Said robbing the stage would be easy as stealing cheese from a blind rat.'

'If things had gone as planned, it would've been.'

'Well, that sure makes me feel better!'

Garrett ignored Avery's sarcasm and helped himself to a cigar from a canister on the desk.

'So, get to the meat. What went wrong?'

Unconcerned, Garrett bit off the end of the cigar, scratched a match against his jeans and calmly lit the tip. 'The guard didn't cooperate, like we expected.'

'Didn't *cooperate*?' Avery's fleshy face reddened until he was almost apoplectic. 'Jesus-goddamn-Christ, Tom, I thought you said he'd already agreed to play along?'

'He did. But at the last minute the bastard got greedy and wanted a bigger share.'

'Wouldn't it have been better to pay him than blast his goddamn guts out?'

'Maybe. But when lead's flying folks don't always make the right decision. Anyway, what's done is done, so there's no use crying over spilt beer.'

Avery gritted his teeth. 'Everything's turning to shit and you're spouting idioms?'

'What would you have me do?' Garrett demanded. 'Fall apart, like you're doing?' Avery had no comeback.

'Things don't always go as planned, Theo. You of all people should know that. If they did, you wouldn't have begged in on this holdup in the first place.'

He was right and Avery sagged in his chair as if punched. 'You swore,' he repeated lamely. 'You gave me your goddamn word.'

'And I meant it when I gave it.'

'I mean, Good God, Tom, if I'd known there'd be shooting I wouldn't have — '

'Wouldn't have *what*, damn you?

Embezzled the money in the first place?'

Again, Avery had no comeback.

'That's the trouble with gutless chiselers like you,' Garrett said angrily. 'You're fine when things are going smooth, but the second there's the slightest hitch, you start whining.'

'I'm not whining.'

'Then what the hell do you call it?' the marshal raged.

Avery flinched. 'Dammit, Tom, keep your voice down. You want everyone in the bank to hear you?' He looked through the window to see if any of the employees were listening. When he saw they weren't, he turned back to the marshal and attempted to mend his bridges. 'Look, I'm not blaming you, Tom. All I'm saying is I took you at your word, so naturally I was very dismayed when I heard about the guard and then saw two of your men gunned down right outside my bank!'

'It's not my fault those dimwits panicked.'

'Why not? They were your men. You hired 'em.'

Unperturbed, Garrett exhaled a stream of blue smoke and studied the glowing tip of the cigar.

'And what's worse,' Avery continued, 'the damn' fools' stuffed their saddlebags with money from the strongbox — money that you and I were counting on!'

'*You* were counting on. To me, it was just another pedigree steer.'

'Regardless, it was still a stupid thing to do. I mean, why'd they show their faces in town to start with?'

'Just following orders.'

'Orders? Whose orders?'

'Mine.'

'*Yours?*'

'Yeah. I wanted to get my hands on that money as soon as possible. Border trash like that, you can't trust them for a second or next thing you know, they're asking themselves why they should turn the money over to us when they took all the goddamn risks. Then you got to spend the rest of your days worrying 'bout being exposed or, worse, getting a bullet in the back.'

Avery, knowing the marshal was right, mopped his brow again and said: 'So what happens now?'

'I go ahead with the original plan like nothing went wrong. The other two guns are waiting for me out at the old Mule Head Mine. I'll ride out there like I planned and get the strongbox — the only difference is I'll have a posse with me.'

'But then the gunmen will know they've been double-crossed.'

'Not until it's too late. I'll have the posse take cover before we get to the mine. I told those two gunnies that no one's been in it since the shaft caved in, so they won't be expecting company. I'll put a bullet in each of them and then call in the boys to help me carry out the strongbox. Having heard the shots they won't be surprised to find the bodies. And if anyone questions me, I'll just say the bandits tried to jump me and I was lucky enough to get the drop on 'em. 'Oh, and by the way, folks, in doing so I saved the bank's money!' The way I figure it, I'll come off looking like a hero.'

'And I'll be your loudest supporter,' Avery said, adding: 'But if that's your plan, why even bother with a posse?'

'I need witnesses.'

'For what?'

'To back up my story. If I ride out there alone, kill the bandits and come back with the strongbox, it might seem too easy, too neat, and maybe arouse suspicion. Some folks might even wonder if I didn't fake the holdup just to make myself look like a hero. But this way, the posse will see me go into the mine, hear the shots and then find the corpses and the strongbox. Hell, when we get back to town I'll even make sure I give them credit for helping me track down the bandits.'

Avery mulled over the marshal's words and then nodded approvingly.

'Just make sure that none of this

spills over onto me, Tom, or I can kiss my chances of ever being governor goodbye.'

'Quit worrying, will you?' Garrett snapped. 'You're in the clear no matter what.'

'I'm also still broke,' Avery reminded. 'Not to mention facing years in prison if I don't repay what I embezzled before the auditors show up.'

'I know a quick solution,' Garrett said. He formed a gun with his hand and pulled an imaginary trigger.

Avery wasn't amused. 'Easy for you to joke around, Tom, you ain't in my shoes.'

'Oh, for God's sake, Theo, pull yourself together, dammit! A few weeks from now, when we hit the Silver Train, you can use your share to pay back what you stole and still have plenty left over to live like a high roller. Hell, in no time at all things will be back to normal.'

'*Normal?*'

'Sure. You'll be rich, like folks think

you are now, and you can run for mayor again, only this time you can buy enough votes to make sure you win. Normal.'

Avery made a scoffing sound. 'If you think this is going to blow over just like that, Tom, then you're *loco*.'

'Why? Once you pay back the bank your hands are clean.'

''Cept for the little matter of the death of a Pinkerton agent.'

'How's that your problem?'

''Cause if the Pinks or the bank directors decide to look into this, which they easily could, they'll bring in Federal marshals and — '

'And what?' Garrett interrupted.

'There'll be a thorough investigation. Can't you see that?'

'So they investigate? So, what? All they got to go on are three dead bodies, two of which were known outlaws and the other a bank guard with a shady past — in other words, dead ends. Soon as the investigators realize that, they'll lose interest faster than money flows through your fingers.'

Avery didn't like the analogy, but at this point he couldn't afford to alienate Garrett, so he tried to sound hopeful as he said: 'Do you honestly believe that, Tom? That we truly are in the clear?'

The lawman snorted derisively. 'If I didn't, do you think I'd be standing here depositing money in your lousy bank, the same goddamn bank we just tried to steal ten thousand dollars from?'

'N-No, I reckon not,' Avery allowed.

'Okay then, pull yourself together! It ain't like we're tenderfoots pissing in the wind. Nothing's going to fly back in our faces. That I promise you.' He smiled and shook Avery's hand for the benefit of anyone watching, turned and left the office.

Avery sank even deeper into his chair, sighed, and tried to relax. It was impossible. His penchant for living beyond his means had made him part of an armed robbery — and three killings — and from now on he'd always be a pawn to be bullied and pushed around by Tom Garrett. And though he knew he had no one to blame but himself, it didn't stop Avery from wishing he had a gun at that moment so he could shoot the marshal and go back to sleeping nights.

13

Melody leaned against the bar in the Silver Spur, idly drinking a beer while he decided what to do next. In all the previous towns when no one had recognized him, he'd drowned his disappointment in a few beers or tequilas and then climbed back in the saddle and ridden on. But thanks to his strong feelings for Regan, and the way she apparently felt about him, he was tempted to break the pattern and stay awhile. Of course, nothing could come of their relationship until he got his memory back. He knew that and he figured she must know it too, even though she'd made it abundantly clear that she didn't want him to leave.

But Regan wasn't the only reason for him to stay: he'd seen the faces of the two gunmen he'd killed and detected more than just fear in their eyes: he also glimpsed recognition. For some reason that thanks to his amnesia he couldn't remember, those bandits had known him.

Unfortunately, he'd had no choice but to gun them down before they killed him. And in doing so, he'd destroyed any chance he might have had to question them and perhaps learn who he was. He smiled bitterly at the irony of the situation. It was almost as if Fate was taunting him, showing him how little control he had over his life, whether it was his past, present or future. Depressing as that was, though, there was also an element of hope to be salvaged from all this: Regan had said there were four men who'd held up the stage. If she was right, and he had no reason to doubt her, perhaps the other two bandits might also recognize him and for a price reveal who he was. It was a long shot, but it was better than no shot at all. All he had to do was track them down and —

The saloon doors swung open, breaking his train of thought, and Marshal Garrett entered. Strutting up to the bar, he drew his Colt and fired once at the ceiling, instantly getting everyone's attention.

'Okay, listen up,' he barked. 'As most of you probably know by now the stage was held up today and the strongbox is missing. Fortunately, half of the stolen money was in the saddlebags of two of the bandits, who this fella' — he thumbed at Melody — 'shot and killed a short while ago.' He paused to let his words sink in; then added dramatically: 'I'm going after the other two and I need volunteers for a posse I'm forming. Now, which of you is coming with me?'

No answer.

'Maybe I didn't make myself clear. This is our town, yours and mine, and we don't want outlaws thinking we're easy pickings. Right?'

More silence.

'And that's what they'll think if we

don't come down hard on these yahoos.'

The men shifted their feet and swapped guilty looks, but still no one said anything.

'I'm telling you true,' Garrett continued. 'If you boys don't back me up and treat these bastards to the wrong end of a rope, word will spread throughout the territory that we're soft and 'fore you can spit oysters, every no-good S.O.B. will be riding in and robbing us blind. Then Silverton won't be a fit place to raise a sow-humping hog in, let alone your young'uns.'

His words hit home and Garrett was encouraged enough by their expressions to continue: 'Now, I know times have been rough lately for some of you boys, and because of that I'll see to it the town council coughs up a few greenbacks to pay you for your efforts. I might even be able to get the Federal Marshal's office to kick in some money — '

'What 'bout a reward?' demanded

one of the men, ' — a percent of how much money's recovered?'

'That's up to the bank, Jake. But I'll try to squeeze something out of them.'

'Just be sure it's enough to pay for a coffin 'case one of us bites the bullet,' another man said.

Instantly, the others around him began clamoring.

'Quiet! Quiet! All of you! Calm down,' the lawman yelled. Then to the speaker: 'No one's going to get shot, Howie. There're only two of them and a whole parcel of us. Capturing or killing them will be easier than greasing a pig. Now,' he added, 'who's coming with me?'

Silence.

Everyone looked at everyone else.

'Count me in,' Melody said, stepping forward. 'I'm new 'round here, but it frosts my tail when a bunch of polecats try to get rich off another man's labor.'

Relieved, the marshal stepped forward and shook Melody's hand.

'Thanks, mister. That's right neighborly of you. Now,' he said to the others, 'who else is signing on or are you going to let a stranger steal your thunder?'

'I'll go,' a third man volunteered.

'Me, too,' chimed in his drinking partner.

'We'll all go,' announced the man who'd spoken first. 'Won't we, boys?'

'Hell, yes,' exclaimed a large bearded man. 'I mean, anything beats having to go home to that ugly shrew wife of mine.'

Everyone laughed. Then finishing their drinks, they all followed the marshal out of the saloon.

Outside, as the men hurried off to get their horses, Garrett grasped Melody's arm.

'I appreciate what you done in there, but what's your real reason for coming?'

'I'm looking for someone,' Melody heard himself say.

'Who?'

Melody, surprised by his last reply, was even more surprised when he said without thinking: 'A roustabout named Wade Colby.'

'Never heard of him,' Garrett said.

'That's not surprising, marshal. Wade ain't worth the holes in his boots.'

'Then why're you looking for him?'

''Cause he pals around with my kid brother. With any luck, one of these bandits might know Wade or know where I can find him and that'll lead me to Luke.'

'Seems odd you need help to find your own brother.'

'Not when you know the whole story.'

'I got nothing but time.'

About to say he couldn't remember why he was looking for his brother, Melody again surprised himself by saying: 'A few years back Luke and me had a falling out and went our own separate ways. We ain't talked since and I'm hoping that when I find him we can mend our fences and bend an elbow together.' As he finished talking, Melody realized this was the first time since regaining consciousness that he'd remembered something from his past, suggesting that his memory was returning. Even more encouraging was the knowledge that he had a younger brother. It gave him a new perspective on life. He no longer felt so alone or lonely. Also, the joy of knowing he had kin so cheered him, he had a hard time maintaining his stoic expression.

But he didn't fool Garrett. The wily veteran sensed a change in Melody and eyed him suspiciously. But when Melody continued to meet his stare without flinching, the marshal lost his belligerence and stuck out his hand. 'Sorry I prodded you, *hombre*.'

'Forget it.'

'It weren't nothing personal, you understand? Just my way of proving to myself that I can trust you — you and everyone else riding with me.'

'Makes sense,' Melody said. 'But you can rest easy, marshal. I'm no back-shooter. Got my word on that and you can take my word to the bank.'

14

Once the men returned with their horses, the fiery little lawman led Melody and the posse out of town in the direction of Seven Mile Bridge.

No one knew why the old trestle-style bridge was so-named, since it was actually located six miles from Silverton. No one could remember exactly when it was built, either, or why it spanned that particular stretch of the river, which was shallow enough to wade across. All they did know was that at every town hall meeting all the nostalgic old timers voted not to change the name of the bridge. The Old West as they knew it, they said, was dying off fast enough without anyone giving it a boost.

Now, despite the late-afternoon heat, the men pushed their horses hard. At the outset Melody, trying to blend in, rode at the rear of the posse. But the marshal waved him forward, insisting that Melody ride up front with him. The men were puzzled by the lawman's gesture. Though everyone in Silverton thought Garrett was a competent lawman, he was known to be unsociable. He was also known to be vindictive and no one in the posse wanted to cross him. Besides, Melody was obviously a man who lived by the gun and the men, most of whom were storekeepers, bartenders or bank workers, were glad to have him on their side.

After the first four miles the horses started laboring. But the marshal didn't let up on the pace and by the time they finally reached the bridge, the weary animals were black with sweat. Melody and the riders weren't in much better shape. Dismounting, they wearily obeyed Garrett's orders and began searching for signs of wheel-marks.

It didn't take long before one man found them. As the others crowded around him, he pointed at the ruts and trampled hoof prints, saying: 'Reckon this is where the stage was held up.'

Everyone nodded in agreement.

'The bandits must've been hiding behind them rocks like Miss Avery said,' put in another man, pointing at some nearby boulders. 'That way, they knew they couldn't be seen by the guard or Hendricks till it was too late.'

'Ben wouldn't have seen 'em even if they were lined up in front of him dancing the can-can,' a third man joked. 'Hell, he's blinder than a bat in broad daylight!'

'Todd's right,' added a fourth man. 'I once rode shotgun with Ben and had to hand him the traces 'cause the S.O.B. couldn't see the brake handle where they was tied!'

'All right, all right, settle down,' Garrett said as everyone laughed. 'We ain't out here for the fun it. We got two renegades to hunt down.'

Melody, who'd been examining the ground near the wheel-ruts, waved the marshal over. 'Reckon they rode off from here. Prints ain't too clear but my guess is they're headed for that mesa.' He pointed toward a large flat-topped hill in the distance.

'Could be you're right,' Garrett admitted. 'But I wouldn't want to bet my spurs on it. Just look around you. There're prints everywhere . . . all heading off in different directions. And any one of them could've been made by the rats we're following. Tell you what,' he added, addressing the posse. 'Reckon our best bet is to split up. Then whichever group catches up with the bastards can signal the rest of us by firing two shots in quick succession.'

The men weren't thrilled about splitting up. It was more dangerous, they grumbled, and wasn't what they'd signed on for. But Garrett stood his ground. Any man who disobeyed him, he warned, would be sent back to town without pay. After a lot of complaining, the men grudgingly split up into four groups and rode off in different directions.

15

At Garrett's insistence, Melody rode with him and the Foley brothers, Deke and Gus. The four of them followed the hoof prints that Melody had pointed out, the trail leading them to the mesa.

Shaped like a man's skull, only with a flat top, it was known as Dead Man's Mesa. Riddled with canyons and ravines filled with abandoned mine shafts and natural caves, it offered ideal hiding places for outlaws and no one from Silverton ever went near it.

'Stay alert,' Garrett warned when they reached the low hills surrounding the mesa. 'There's renegades hiding in those caves. Keep your eyes peeled or you'll be asking to be picked off.'

The tracks led them between two of the smaller hills, neither of which had any caves or mines, on into a narrow ravine with steep sandstone cliffs on both sides. The side on Melody's left was so sheer its only inhabitants were birds. As he rode beside the marshal, Melody spotted their nests in the numerous crannies and ledges dotting the face. The other side, to the right of the Foleys, wasn't as steep and there were natural footpaths leading up to the lower, more-accessible caves.

'Fan out,' Garrett ordered. 'Gus . . . Deke,' he added, 'you two ride close to the caves and if anything moves, shoot it.'

The brothers' scowls showed they weren't happy about offering themselves as targets, but as former Union soldiers they were too disciplined to disobey orders.

To Melody, it seemed like Garrett was deliberately trying to get the Foleys killed. But unable to figure out what the marshal's motives were, he kept his thoughts to himself and decided to wait and watch.

The four of them continued to ride cautiously through the ravine. Other than a few lizards and desert pocket mice, and a sluggish sidewinder crossing their path, nothing eventful happened until they were about halfway through; then Melody glimpsed a flash of light in the mouth of one of the lower caves. Guessing it was the sunlight reflecting off the barrel of a rifle or a pistol, he reined up and dismounted.

His abrupt move caught the others off-guard and they rode on for a short distance before realizing that Melody wasn't with them. Then all three reined up, but only Garrett returned beside Melody.

'What's wrong?' he demanded.

'He's picked up a stone,' Melody said, indicating the bay. 'You three ride on ahead and I'll catch up with you soon as I dig it out.' He spoke loud enough to be heard by anyone in the lower caves and before the marshal could reply, added softly: 'It may be nothing, but I think our friends are hiding in that narrow cave over my left shoulder.'

Garrett, savvy enough not to look at the cave, whispered: 'Do they got a bead on us now?'

Melody gave the faintest of nods. 'Rifle looks like, yeah.'

'Make it fast,' Garrett said loudly. 'We don't want to be out here at sundown.'

'Will do, marshal. But if it's a loose shoe, I'll have to call it quits and head back to town to see the blacksmith.'

It took a moment for Garrett to catch on. Then he said, 'Do what you must, deputy,' wheeled his horse around and rode back to the Foley brothers.

Melody watched as the three men continued on, then kneeled down and examined the bay's left front hoof. He took his time, eventually drawing his knife and pretending to dig out a stone from the shoe. As he worked, he managed to take several quick looks under the horse's belly at the cave where he'd seen the reflected sunlight.

His deception worked. The third time

he looked he saw loose dirt sliding down the slope beneath the cave as one of the bandits shifted his rifle. Satisfied, Melody stood up and cursed the bay for cheating him out of his share of the reward money. He then grasped the reins and led the horse back toward the entrance of the ravine.

Ahead, the trail disappeared around a pile of rocks that had been dislodged from the slope by blasting powder. Melody looked above the rocks and farther up the slope saw an old mine entrance and derelict wooden sluice, all that were left of a miner's dream.

He continued walking until he was behind the rocks, then grabbed his rifle and scrambled up to the abandoned mine. Once there, he crawled between the rocks until he could see the bandits' cave. Resting his Winchester on a rock, he aimed at the entrance. He hadn't long to wait. Unaware that they were being watched, the bandits stood up and looked off after Garrett and the Foley brothers. The three men had almost reached the far end of the ravine. The bandits, believing they were free, ducked back into the cave and reappeared shortly with the strongbox.

Melody kept his rifle sights on them and waited to see what would happen next.

The bandits tied a rope to one of the handles of the strongbox then paid out the rope so that the box slid down the slope ahead of them. Once the rope was fully extended, they slowly descended the slope, repeating the process until they and the strongbox reached the bottom. There they quickly carried the box behind a pile of rocks. Melody patiently continued to watch and wait.

Shortly the bandits reappeared on horseback. They no longer had the strongbox but now their saddlebags bulged with stolen money. After a final look at the marshal and the Foley brothers, who were now riding out of the far end of the ravine, the bandits spurred their horses toward the entrance.

Melody waited until they were directly below him. Then, resisting the urge to kill them, he fired a warning shot that kicked up dirt in front of the horses.

Startled, both bandits reined up and reached for their six-guns.

A second shot knocked the hat from the nearest bandit.

'Sky 'em,' Melody called out. 'Or one of you dies.'

Grudgingly, the bandits raised their hands.

Melody rose, and keeping his Winchester aimed at the bandits descended the slope.

On seeing him the bandits at first looked surprised and then relieved. One of them, a large man with an unkempt red beard, said: 'What the hell you doing, J. T.? Don't you know we're in on this?'

'In on what?' Melody said.

Before Red Beard could reply, his hatless partner, a small man with no teeth, said: 'We don't got time for games.'

Melody cocked the hammers of his shotgun. 'Does it look like I'm playing games?'

'Then what — ?' began No Teeth.

Red Beard cut him off. 'Hang on, Lee. Maybe there's been a change of plans. Is that right, J. T.? Has the marshal — ?'

'Shut your goddamn yap!' No Teeth snarled. Then to Melody: 'The short of it is, Red and me, we got the rest of the money from the strongbox in our saddlebags. Soon as we're gone, turn them over to Marshal Garrett!'

Melody looked toward the far end of the ravine and saw Garrett and the Foley brothers riding toward him. 'Before you go, gents, how 'bout telling me what J. T. stands for?'

The bandits exchanged puzzled looks.

'What the hell you talking about?' said No Teeth.

'J. T,' said Melody. 'What're they short for?'

'Quit funning around, will you?' Red Beard growled.

'Tell me,' Melody said, 'or I swear you'll dance from a rope.'

'Judas Trask, of course!'

'*Judas?*'

Red Beard shrugged. 'Why do you think you always go by J. T.?'

Melody repeated the name but it didn't conjure up any images, frustrating him.

'Either of you got any idea where I'm from?'

'I don't know what kind of game you're playing,' snarled No Teeth, 'but — '

Melody stopped him. 'Just tell me, damn you.'

'The Panhandle. Amarillo, maybe.'

'Plainview,' corrected Red Beard. ''Least, that's what Wade Colby told me.'

Melody glimpsed images of a cabin, barn and corrals surrounded by open plains. Everything was in flames. Then those images blurred and turned into a familiar image picturing the inside of the barn . . .

At first all seemed normal. Then horrific images flashed through his mind. A wall spattered with blood, nearby a dead woman with torn clothes and numerous cuts and bruises lay sprawled on the hay in a stall . . . and not far away more gory blood spatters that led to two small girls, lying in their own blood. Melody sensed he knew them, but couldn't recall who they were. Though they were dead the voices of all the corpses kept screaming and screaming until his mind threatened to explode. Then everything faded and he heard himself say: 'This Colby — when'd you last see him?'

'Month ago, maybe two.'

'Where?'

'Near the border. He was with your kid brother. Said they was headed for Laredo to chase the rabbit and get shit-assed drunk.'

Before Melody could respond, No Teeth exclaimed angrily: 'If you're all done asking damn' fool questions, J. T., for chrissake let us ride.'

Melody saw Garrett and the Foleys closing in, said: 'Drop your saddlebags first!'

The bandits stood up in the stirrups, pulled their saddlebags from under the cantels and tossed them to Melody. They landed at his feet. He made no attempt to pick them up, but kept his Winchester trained on the bandits as they spurred their horses away.

Minutes later Garrett and the Foleys galloped up. The marshal jerked his horse to a sliding stop, while the brothers raced on after the bandits.

'You better have a good reason for letting them gunnies go,' Garrett told Melody. 'Or your next meal comes served with a rope!'

'Little late for posturing,' Melody said disgustedly. 'Your partners just sold you out to save their own damn necks.'

Garrett ignored the threat. Dismounting, he grabbed his rifle, rested the barrel across his saddle, aimed carefully at the fleeing bandits and squeezed the trigger.

His first bullet knocked Red Beard off his horse. The outlaw landed, flopped over onto his back and lay still. Garrett's second shot missed its target but brought down the horse, sending No Teeth flying over its head. He landed and went sprawling.

Garrett snapped off a third shot.

No Teeth was struggling to get up when the marshal's bullet tore away part of his head. Blood sprayed everywhere. No Teeth slumped forward onto the dirt.

Melody sarcastically clapped his hands. 'Nice shooting, marshal. Guess you ain't planning on sharing the reward money.'

Pissed, Garrett swung around and jabbed his rifle into Melody's belly. 'That reason — I'd like to hear it now.'

'You already know it,' Melody said.

'Humor me.'

'Like I said, I swapped their lives for the rest of the money from the holdup — *if* you can call it a holdup!'

'What's that supposed to mean?'

'You tell me. You're the one in cahoots with the bandits.'

Garrett gave a scoffing laugh. 'Got a pot of gold to go with that rainbow?'

'I did — till you killed the last two men who could tie you to the holdup. Smart move, by the way.'

Garrett's finger tightened on the trigger. 'You must enjoy taking risks, *hombre*.'

'So must you, if you're partnering with crow bait like those cheap gunnies.'

For an instant Garrett looked as if he might pull the trigger. Then he suddenly laughed and lowered the rifle. 'Know something, J. T.? You're full of hot air.'

'Possibly,' said Melody. 'But even if I'm not, and could dig up some dirt on you, you got no call to worry.'

'No? Why's that?'

'Because it ain't my nature to poke my nose in other folks' business.'

'What if someone prods you 'bout

letting the bandits escape?'

'I'll just tell him that I can't hit the side of a freight car with a rifle.'

'More hot air.'

'Know something I don't, do you?'

Garrett smiled wolfishly. 'Just that a fella in El Paso once told me you can shoot the eye out of an eagle on the wing.'

'Exaggeration,' Melody deadpanned. ' — tis a pure and wondrous thing.'

'The fella I'm thinking of ain't known for exaggerating or bending the truth.'

'Ezra Macahan,' Melody said fondly. 'Solid as four aces.'

'None better.' Garrett paused as he saw the Foleys riding toward them, each brother leading a horse with a dead bandit draped over the saddle, then added: 'As for the reward money, I intend to see that every man on the posse gets an equal share.'

'Including me?' Melody needled.

'*Especially* you.'

'I can't wait to hear why.'

''Cause I'm retiring soon and I'm

going to recommend you for my job.'

Melody laughed sourly. 'Now why the hell would I want to be marshal?'

'So you can retire in a few years with a nest egg, same as me.'

'On a town marshal's wages?'

'Forget wages. They don't count for spit. It's the money I get under the table that makes being marshal pay off.'

'Money under the — ?'

'From Theo Avery.'

'Regan's father?'

'The same. We have a deal. Fifty-fifty split of everything he skims off the top of the bank's profits and any money we make from holding up the stage now and then.'

Melody stared at the marshal, trying to figure out if he was serious or joking.

Garrett, as if reading his mind, said: 'How do you think I was able to buy a spread near Tucson and stock it with good Texas beef?'

'I didn't even know you had a ranch.'

'It ain't something I advertise,' Garrett admitted.

'This deal with Avery?' Melody said after a pause. 'How's his daughter fit into it?'

'She don't. According to Avery, she's so straight-laced, if she ever found out that he was juggling the books at the bank she'd turn him in.'

Relieved, Melody said: 'So why are you telling me all this?'

'I just told you: I'm retiring soon and with your record, I figured you'd make a good replacement.'

'Record?'

'Don't play dumb with me, cowboy. From the Wanted Posters that I've seen from time to time, you ain't exactly what I'd call a model citizen.'

'Those are old posters. There's no paper out on me now.'

'Once a thief, always a thief. 'Sides, this is a perfect set up for you. Hell, where else can you steal money without gunplay?'

Melody knew he was right. 'What 'bout Avery?' he asked. 'Surely he's got some say in who becomes his partner?'

'Don't worry about Avery. He'll do as I tell him. He may talk a good fight, but he's got no grit when it comes to making tough decisions. Hell, without my backbone and this star on my chest to support him, he'd have trouble getting out of bed.'

Melody didn't say anything.

'Well, what do you think?' Garrett pressed. 'You interested?'

'Sure.'

'Good. I'll talk to Avery and let you know when he wants to have a sit-down.'

'Just make sure it's not for a couple of weeks. I got some personal business to take care of and I don't know exactly how long it's going to take.'

'Fair enough. In the meantime, keep this under your hat. Don't breathe a word to anyone. And that includes Avery's daughter, who I know you're sweet on.'

'Don't worry,' Melody said. 'She'll be the last to know.'

Garrett, noticing the Foley brothers

returning, swung up in the saddle. 'Stay alive, *hombre*.'

'You too.' Melody watched as Garrett galloped away. Mind churning, he tried to convince himself that this was a golden opportunity for him. All he had to do was make sure that Regan never found out. Because if she did, he knew he'd lose her. And right now, that was the last thing he wanted.

16

At sunset that evening, with the warm night air filled with whining mosquitoes, Regan sat in a swing-chair on the front porch of her home and tried not to be depressed as Melody told her he was leaving.

'How long will you be gone?' she asked when he was finished. 'Do you know?'

'A month, maybe.'

'I see.'

'Don't be sore at me.'

'I'm not. I — '

'You *do* want me to get my memory back, don't you?'

'Of course,' Regan said. 'I just don't see why you have to go all the way to Plainview to do that.'

''Cause that's where I'm from and I figure that's where it all started.'

'Why? Have you remembered something that happened?'

'No. But I keep seeing images. They're just glimpses, you understand, but they take place at my home in Plainview, so I figure I ought to go back there and see if anything there helps jog my memory.'

'These images,' Regan said, 'what're they like?'

'That's the problem,' he said, 'they're so blurred and jumbled together they don't make sense.'

'But you think they're connected to you?'

'Possibly.'

'That's a long way to ride on 'possibly'.'

'I know. But until I get my memory back and find out exactly who I am and what caused me to lose it in the first place, I can't get on with my life. And that includes being with you.'

Regan thought a moment before asking: 'The images — are they good or bad?'

'Melody shrugged. 'Like I said, they're too blurred and jumbled for me to tell. They also come and go so fast, I don't have time to figure out what's real and what isn't.' He paused, and not wanting to upset her by describing the gory images he'd seen, said: 'For all I know I may be losing touch with reality and none of it's real.'

'Are you implying that you're going crazy?'

'I don't know what I'm implying. But it's possible, ain't it?'

'Anything's possible. Doesn't mean it's true, though.'

'Maybe not,' Melody said. 'But true or not, I still have to get my memory back 'fore I can get on with my life. And that's what I plan on doing.'

Regan sighed, unconvinced. 'Well, if you believe you have to go, then of course you must. But I wish you'd reconsider — hold off going for another month or so.'

'Why? What would be different in a month?'

'Maybe nothing. Medicine isn't an exact science. It's mostly trial and error.

But having you here would give me time to research your condition more thoroughly . . . possibly even find a way to break down the block that's preventing you from remembering your past.'

Tempted, Melody hesitated before saying: 'It's mighty kind of you to offer to help me and I probably should take you up on it, but I can't. Loco as it sounds, something's pulling on me, insisting I go to Plainview and face whatever's waiting for me there.'

'Very well . . . ' Regan dabbed the tears from her eyes with a lace handkerchief. 'Just know that I'll be waiting for you when you get back.'

'You will?'

'Yes. But you must promise me one thing. No,' she added as he started to interrupt, 'don't say anything. Just listen. Let me do the talking.'

Melody fell silent, at the same time feeling guilty for not telling Regan about how crooked her father was. The trouble was he knew she'd never want to see him again and like he'd told

Garrett, that wasn't what he wanted.

' . . . if at any time while you're gone you change your mind regarding how feel about me,' he heard Regan saying, 'or you find someone else that you'd rather be with, then please have the decency to tell me to my face.' She paused and needed a moment to gather herself before adding: 'That way, I won't waste my life waiting for someone who no longer loves me. Will you promise me that, Melody?'

'Got my solemn word on it.'

'Thank you,' Regan said softly. Tears sparkled in her eyes but they were tears of happiness. 'Now I don't mind waiting . . . no matter how long as it takes.'

He couldn't find the words to express himself, so he did the only thing he could think of: he kissed her.

17

He rode out of town with the taste of her mouth on his lips. He was sure Regan wasn't the first or only woman he'd ever kissed, but for the time being she was the only one he remembered. She was far from the painted women in the recent dancehalls he'd recently frequented, but the faint smell of her powder lingered in his nostrils and he found it most pleasurable. Dog tired, he sat slumped forward in the saddle, the smooth loping gait of the bay under him threatening to lull him to sleep.

As he rode across the moon-whitened wasteland he saw a rider approaching in the distance. He was leading four horses, each with a corpse draped over the saddle, and as he got closer Melody realized it was Marshal Garrett!

Melody reined up. Wary now, he rested one hand on his six-gun and watched as the little lawman rode toward him. As he waited, Melody shifted his gaze to the corpses. Two of them belonged to the bandits. No surprise there. But the other two dead men were the Foley brothers! Shocked, Melody controlled his emotions and remained still as stone in the middle of the trail.

It took a while but finally Garrett reined up in front of him. ''Evening, son.'

'Marshal.'

'Leaving town?'

'For a spell.'

'Where you headed?'

'Texas.'

'Where in Texas?'

'No place in particular,' Melody lied. 'Why?'

'Reward money. I need to know where to send your share.'

'Hang on to it, marshal. I'll collect it when I get back.'

'Consider it done,' the lawman said. 'Well, ride safe, *hombre*.'

'Always.' Melody eyed the bodies of the Foley brothers. 'Looks like they could've used your advice.'

'I gave 'em fair warning,' Garrett said. 'Told those boys to keep their eyes peeled or they'd get picked off by renegades. But then the Foleys, they never did care much for another man's advice.'

Melody, noticing the blood on the back of each brother's shirt, said wryly: 'Even the best advice can't save a fella from a bullet in the back.'

'True,' agreed Garrett. 'Trick is to never let anyone get behind you.'

'Not even folks you trust?'

'*Especially* not them! Trust and friendship, hell, they only make a man vulnerable.'

'Careful,' Melody needled, 'or folks might think you're getting a tad cynical.'

Garrett chuckled and nudged his horse forward. 'So long, son. Try to stay alive.'

As the lawman rode past him,

Melody prepared to draw if Garrett made a move to shoot him like he'd surely shot the Foley brothers. But the marshal kept his hands in sight, whistling cheerfully, and was soon swallowed up by the darkness.

Relieved, Melody kicked up the bay and continued riding southeast toward the Panhandle.

18

Officially, Plainview was named after the unobstructed view of the vast prairie that surrounded the little town. But according to legend, the reason was more colorful: its name derived from an amusing incident involving a local old timer. Needing to relieve himself but unable to find any cover, he peed out in the open, causing his pals to remark: 'Look, he's going in plain view!'

Like most cow towns and settlements that took root in the Panhandle in the late 1870s, early 1880s, it was founded by a few brave settlers who were willing to face scorching summers, freezing winters and marauding Comanches in order to build their log cabins and clapboard houses on a dirt street or around a public square. There was no shortage of free land, but constant Indian attacks scared off most ranchers and farmers, preventing the population from growing. It wasn't until 1874-'75, after Colonel 'Bad Hand' Mckenzie's forces had won several decisive victories — the last being the Battle of Palo Duro Canyon — that the proud but defeated Comanches were forced to live on a reservation.

With the Indian threat all but gone, other settlers soon found the courage to build outlying ranches on the wind-swept prairie, supporting their families by hunting buffalo and antelope and rounding up wild mustangs that when broken were shipped by the Southern Kansas Railway Company — then a subsidiary of the mighty Santa Fe — to the various military forts in the territory where they were sold at a considerable profit to the U.S. Army.

Though land was plentiful timber was scarce and as Plainview slowly grew, newcomers were forced to have their lumber freighted from Amarillo. Because of this additional expense, in the early years there were only a few substantial buildings in town and each one of those had to serve double duty.

Now, though, in the late '80s, as Melody rode into town, Plainview's population had grown big enough to support a separate school, courthouse, church, mercantile store, two saloons and a post-office. He'd hoped that by returning to his home town and seeing the various buildings and streets, they would help restore his memory or at least stir up a few recollections of his past; but as he rode along the main street nothing seemed familiar. And no new images came to mind.

Yet by the way passersby stopped and stared at him, first surprised then alarmed, and then hurried off Melody knew that at least everyone recognized him.

Puzzled by their obvious fear of him, he dismounted and tied up his horse outside the larger of the two saloons, The First Chance. He stood there for a few moments in the hot sun, warily watching as everyone hurriedly crossed over to avoid him, and then entered the saloon. The abrupt change from brilliant sunlight to a barroom dimly lit by kerosene lamps temporarily blinded him and he was forced to stand just inside the entrance until his eyes adjusted to the lack of light.

Once he could see, he joined the customers drinking at the long polished bar and looked around. Facing him men sat playing poker at smoky, lantern-lit tables while others tried their luck at roulette or the craps table.

Melody sensed he'd been here before — but when and in what capacity eluded him. He ordered a whiskey from a gaunt, nervous bartender and pretended not to notice that the men along the bar were retreating. His eyes strayed to the large painting behind the bar. The scene looked familiar and as he stared at it, he realized it resembled the same river and rapids from which he'd rescued Regan.

Surprised, he closed his eyes and tried to remember exactly what the canyon on both sides of the river looked like. Once he had a picture locked in his mind, he opened his eyes and studied the painting. There was no mistake. The artist had painted the picture somewhere in the canyon. About to inquire if anyone knew the artist, Melody suddenly realized that most of the customers had already hurried out and the barkeep was pulling his apron over his head, also intending to leave.

'Hold it!' Melody growled at him. Then as the bartender froze: 'What the hell's going on? Why's everyone scooting out of here?'

The barkeep cringed. 'Please, Mr. Trask, don't shoot me. I got a wife and three young'uns who depend on me and — '

Melody stopped him. 'Why the hell would I want to shoot you? You — or anyone else 'round here?'

'I . . . I dunno, sir.'

Melody sensed he was lying and wondered why.

'You'd better start remembering,' he warned, ''cause I want to know why the whole town is acting like they're scared to death of me. Everywhere I go, soon as folks see me, they run like I got the plague or something. Where's the sense in that?'

'I . . . I . . . honestly couldn't say, Mr. Trask,' the barkeep stammered. 'I'm new here and I've never seen you before, so I can't help you.'

'If you never saw me before how'd you know my name?'

The bartender looked at him as if he were joking. 'Everybody knows who you are, sir. Why, even my wife, she keeps our boys in line by threatening to have you punish them if they don't do their chores.'

Melody could only shake his head in disbelief.

'M-May I go now, please, Mr. Trask?'

'I'll save you the trouble,' Melody said. He gulped down his drink and walked out.

As he stepped out into the bright

sunlight, he found himself confronted by four men, all pointing shotguns at him.

Melody froze.

A big-bellied middle-aged man in jeans and a denim shirt with shoulder-length black curls and a sheriff's star pinned on his vest brandished a shotgun at him. 'Keep your hand away from your gun,' he warned, 'or we'll be forced to shoot you!'

Melody raised his hands and studied the lawman, whose angry face looked vaguely familiar. 'I'd be obliged if you'd tell me what this is about,' he said quietly.

'You got the goddamn gall to ask *me* that?' Sheriff Frank Dordoff raged. 'Hell's fire, J. T., I ought to kill you, you gutless murdering sonofabitch, just for daring to show up here!'

''Fore you do that,' Melody said, 'I got a right to know who it was I murdered.'

It was the wrong thing to say. Unable to control his rage any longer the sheriff stepped close and slammed him across the head with his shotgun.

The last thing Melody remembered was an explosion of tiny lights behind his eyes. Then darkness engulfed him and he knew no more.

19

When he regained consciousness, Melody found himself lying in the dark on the dirt floor of a small sod house. There were no windows. The only light came from a faint crack showing along the bottom of the strap-hinged door.

Not knowing how long he'd been out, he slowly sat up. The movement made him dizzy. Worse, it increased the painful throbbing in his head and Melody gave a stifled groan. He gingerly felt the side of his head where he'd been struck by the sheriff's shotgun. It was swollen and bruised and even the lightest touch caused excruciating pain. Fearing he might vomit, he sat very still until the pain lessened and the sickness gradually went away.

While he waited blurred images

flashed through his mind. Like before they blended together so rapidly he found it almost impossible to tell one from another, or to fully comprehend what it was he was seeing. One thing he did realize though: like most of the previous images they took place inside a barn and were horrific. Sickened by them, he tried to distinguish the stabbed and bleeding bodies and brutally battered faces looking at him from the blood-soaked hay. It took great concentration but finally he mentally slowed the images enough to realize they were the same dead woman and two young girls he'd visualized before. All three stared at him, their bulging eyes and tortured expressions depicting the prolonged agony they had experienced before mercifully dying.

Melody shuddered and blinked in an effort to get rid of the images. It worked. When he closed his eyes again the images had vanished. But in their place was something else, something unexpected: his memory!

It didn't return gradually, as he'd expected, but came back as suddenly as it had disappeared, so that without warning he went from having no memory to vividly remembering everything — including the identity of the dead woman and two young girls that had been haunting him.

They were his wife, Meryl and daughters, Catherine and Elizabeth!

Momentarily, the realization was so horrific that his mind refused to accept it. Then when he could no longer block out the truth, it hit him with such impact that he groaned aloud.

Desperate, he again tried to reject the devastating images by telling himself that they were merely the after effect of a horrible nightmare. When that lie didn't work, he combed his memory for an acceptable reason for the gory images he'd just seen. But that didn't work either, because every time he closed his eyes, all he saw was blood running down behind his lids. Opening his eyes, he continued to sit there, numbly trying to remember everything pertaining to his wife and daughters, in no particular order, and then tried to connect those jumbled thoughts to their grisly death.

But there was no connection; or none that Melody could think of. His last memory of his wife and daughters was a pleasant one. He remembered kissing Meryl goodbye in the doorway of their log cabin, and then playfully trying to catch the girls as they ran, giggling and screaming, around inside the fenced yard, their dog barking at their heels, chickens scattering before them.

It was a game he always played with his daughters whenever he was going to be gone hunting for a few days. He could have caught them within moments, but that would have ruined the game, for him and for the girls. So he lumbered around the yard after them, arms outstretched like an angry grizzly, making exaggerated growling noises that made them laugh and scream even louder.

Finally, when he was winded and still hadn't caught them, he sank to his knees, gasping, and then flopped onto his back. This was the part he and the girls loved best. Both pounced on him, laughing shrilly and calling him unflattering names. He briefly endured their abuse then suddenly bear-hugged them until they begged for mercy.

Now, though, even as he mentally hugged his daughters, their battered and bleeding faces flashed before him, this time refusing to go away no matter how many times he blinked. And if that wasn't ugly enough, the face of his wife, equally swollen and bloody, floated above the girls' heads, her pain-filled eyes begging whoever was hurting her to stop.

Mingled in with the playful shrieks of his daughters was a prolonged scream that at first he didn't recognize. But as it grew louder and louder, he realized that the scream was coming from him. Shocked, he clapped his hands over his mouth, muffling the sound until gradually it faded altogether and he realized he'd stopped.

At the same instant the door was unbolted and jerked open and a man's silhouette stood in the doorway, framed by the daylight behind him.

'So, you finally decided to wake up, huh?' Deputy Elvin Fisk said. 'It's about time! I was ready to throw cold water over you. Not that any of us would've given a damn whether you was awake or not,' he added. 'But apparently it's against the law to hang someone who's unconscious — even a murdering rat like you!'

'What about a trial?' Melody said through his swollen and bloodied lips.

'Trial?'

'Don't I get one?'

'What for? Hell, everyone knows you murdered your wife and girls.'

'How do they know?' Melody demanded.

''Cause you were caught red-handed, that's why.'

'By who?'

'Sheriff Dordoff. He found you standing over the bodies in the barn, their blood all over you!'

'If Dordoff says that, he's an even bigger liar than I figured,' Melody said.

'Why would he lie 'bout something like that?'

''Cause he hates my guts. Everybody knows that.'

'That still don't mean he wasn't there,' Deputy Fisk said, adding: 'Maybe you just don't want to remember him on account of what you did?'

'I didn't *do* anything, damn you! And Frank knows it. What's more, he knows he ain't welcome at my home, so what was he doing there? Anyone think to ask that?'

'Jesus, you must be as ignorant as you look!' Fisk said. He moved closer and Melody saw the deputy sheriff star pinned on his vest. 'Since when does a brother need a reason to visit his own sister and nieces!'

'First off,' Melody said angrily,

'Frank Dordoff is — or was Meryl's stepbrother, not brother. Secondly, they ain't seen eye-to-eye since they were young'uns. That's why she left home while still a young'un — so she wouldn't have to put up with him mauling her every chance he got.'

'I know nothing 'bout that,' said Fisk.

'And lastly,' Melody continued, 'it was Meryl who made it perfectly clear to Frank that he was never to come to our home! Not under any circumstances! So you can see, can't you, why I want to know what the lecherous sonofabitch was doing there!'

Deputy Fisk, clearly intimidated by Melody, took a step back, saying: 'That's something you'll have to take up with Sheriff Dordoff.'

'I'll be happy to,' Melody said, 'if the no-good bastard has the nerve to face me.'

'He's got no choice. Being sheriff, he has to be present at your hanging.'

'Great,' Melody said. 'I can spit on the S.O.B. just 'fore the trap's sprung.'

Fisk moved to the doorway, where he paused and gave Melody a puzzled look. 'Talking of hanging, J. T., there's something I'd like to know — me and everybody else in town.'

'What's that?'

'You seem like a smart fella, so what the hell made you do it?'

''Mean, come back here?'

'You knew you were facing a rope, so whatever possessed you to do such a damn fool thing?'

'I had my reasons,' Melody growled.

'Like, what?'

'They're personal. Now, get the hell out of here and leave me in peace!'

'With pleasure.' Deputy Fisk slammed the door and slid the bolt in place.

20

Alone in the darkness Melody went over everything again in his mind. But despite carefully sifting through all the details, the last happy images of his wife and daughters as he bid them goodbye remained unchanged.

As for the hunt, he remembered that it had gone well. On only the second day out he tracked down a nice fat doe and killed it with his first shot. Returning to his camp, he skinned it out, cutting up the meat and wrapping it in the tarp he'd brought along and then tying it onto the back of his horse.

The bay was unhappy about the smell of fresh blood being so close and became more skittish than usual. As Melody fought to hobble it for the night, he wondered if he'd made a mistake by not trading his Sharps for his neighbor's packhorse. The deal they had discussed was fair, but he'd owned the gun for years and at the time felt that to get rid of it would be like betraying an old friend.

His mind shifted from his camp to the ride home. Normally, a hunt took several days and nights and Melody, eager to be back with his family, would have pushed the bay to its limits. But having been gone for only two days, he rode at a more leisurely pace and once out of the hills and on the flatlands, instead of racing home decided that since the evening was so beautiful, he'd sleep under the stars.

He chose a hollow sheltered by boulders, spread out his bedroll and started a fire.

Coffee was soon boiling in the pot hanging over the flames. Normally he would have eaten the jerky he'd brought along, but to celebrate his hunting luck he instead cut a steak from the loin of the doe, rubbed it with hickory chips and molasses that he kept in his pack and pan-fried it. He cooked it quickly, so that the meat was tender and sweet, and after he'd eaten lay there on his back, head resting on his saddle, staring at the glittering heavens, wondering how he managed to be this lucky.

He didn't remember falling asleep; only waking up in the chill of dawn. Shivering as he relieved himself, he then stirred the embers and reheated the coffee, gulping it down so its bitterness didn't linger in his mouth. Lastly, he packed everything up, saddled the bay and started home.

When still a mile or so from the cabin, he passed three bearded, sour-faced drifters who were riding in a westerly direction. He exchanged nodded greetings with them, thinking as he did that he'd never seen them before — which was surprising because he was friendly with all his neighbors as well as almost everyone in town.

But knowing that the wide-open territory was still attracting outsiders, he didn't give the drifters much thought. Besides, now that he was almost home he could think of little else but his wife and daughters and how glad they'd be to see him; especially when they saw he'd killed enough meat to last them through the upcoming winter.

The cabin was now in sight. He could see washing drying like so many white flags on the new clothesline that Meryl had nagged him to string up for her. He swelled with pride and happiness . . .

Then suddenly, without warning, his mind went blank. Surprised, he opened his eyes and peered about him in the darkness. The thin bar of light under the door was brighter than before, reminding him that the day was passing and his inevitable walk to the gallows was drawing ever-closer.

On the other side of the door he heard muffled voices. He couldn't hear what they were saying, but after a few minutes they stopped and he heard the bolt slide back. A moment later the door swung open. Glaring sunlight flooded in, forcing Melody to squint and shade his eyes.

21

Sheriff Dordoff entered. Behind him Deputy Fisk stood in the doorway, covering Melody with a shotgun.

'Get up and stand against the wall,' Dordoff ordered. 'Don't move,' he warned as Melody obeyed him. 'That's unless, of course, you'd sooner die from a belly load of buckshot than dangling from a rope.'

Melody kept silent while promising himself that if he got the chance, he'd grab Dordoff and snap his neck.

The sheriff eyed Melody with intense hatred and disgust. 'My deputy tells me that you don't believe I was at your cabin the day you murdered your family?'

'I would've remembered if you were, Frank. Trust me on that.'

'I wouldn't trust you under any cir-cumstances,' Dordoff said contemptuously.

'But I'm here to tell you that your memory's gone south on you, J. T. I was there, sure as I'm standing here before you!'

'You saying it, Frank, don't make it Gospel. But let's table that and get to a more important question: Why were you there in the first place? Meryl made it real clear you weren't welcome, so why don't you tell me what reason you had for coming out?'

'First off,' Dordoff growled, 'I don't have to tell you nothing. I'm sheriff and you're a murdering swine about to do a death dance — which, I might add, I can't wait to watch. But because it's a pleasure telling you why I was at your cabin, I'll humor you with my reason. It was because my sister — '

'*Step*-sister — '

'Meryl, wanted me there.'

'That's a goddamn lie and you know it.'

'Is it? Then how come I have a note from her asking me to protect her while she and the girls packed up their things and moved into town?'

'Bullshit!' Melody said. 'Meryl wouldn't ask you for help if she and the girls were *drowning*!'

Dordoff laughed tauntingly. 'I knew that's what you'd say. My God, J. T. you're so predictable.'

'Then you can probably predict what I'm going to say next: show me the note, so I can tell if it is Meryl's writing or not.'

'Sorry, I don't have it.'

'Frank, I got a legal right to see it.'

'Right? *Right*? What 'bout my sister's rights and the rights of my nieces? Where were their rights when you cut them to pieces?'

'Frank, I didn't — '

'Shut up, damn you, or I'll shoot you myself and save the hangman his job.'

Melody grudgingly fell silent.

'As for the note,' Dordoff continued, 'it's evidence now — proof that you had a motive for murdering Meryl and the girls — and I turned it over to the court. Oh, and just so you don't die wondering why you don't remember me being at your cabin, the reason is because you were falling down drunk. Seems you so enjoyed stabbing Meryl and the girls to death you decided to celebrate. Go ahead,' he said as Melody seemed about to attack him. 'My deputy's just itching to turn that scattergun loose on you.'

Melody somehow managed to control himself.

'That's another lie,' he said grimly. 'I wasn't drunk and you know it. Hell, up until a few days ago I hadn't had a drink in over six months — not since I promised Meryl I'd go on the wagon.'

'You and your promises can go to hell,' Dordoff said. 'I know what I saw and what I saw was you standing there in the barn, bottle in one hand, knife in the other, reeking of whiskey.'

'He's telling it to you true,' Deputy Fisk told Melody. 'You stunk so bad when he brought you in, we had to clean you up 'fore we could throw you in jail.'

He sounded so sincere that Melody

wondered if he really had been drunk and didn't remember it, even now that he'd gotten his memory back. Before he could decide, the sheriff checked his time piece and turned to his deputy.

'It's time, Fisk. Put wrist-irons on the prisoner and bring him to the gallows.'

Deputy Fisk handed Dordoff his shotgun, unhooked his wrist-irons from his belt and told Melody to turn around and put his hands behind his back. When Melody obeyed him, Fisk cautiously approached and locked the irons around his wrists. Then drawing his Colt, he jammed it in Melody's back and prodded him to the door.

Dordoff, keeping the shotgun aimed at Melody, backed out of the door ahead of them.

Once outside, Dordoff continued to keep the shotgun trained on Melody as he walked abreast of him. The threesome crossed the walled compound fronting the sod house jail, stopping only when they reached the steps leading up to the gallows. Two other armed deputies guarding the wooden entrance gate looked on intently as Melody climbed the steps, with Fisk close behind him.

On reaching the platform Melody paused next to the trapdoor in the floor.

'Move over,' Fisk said. He pushed Melody onto the trapdoor, the hangman's noose now hanging beside his neck.

A large, hulking man in black, wearing a hood with cutouts for his eyes, labored up the steps and stopped in front of Melody. He none-too-gently looped the noose over Melody's head, pulled it tight so that the hangman's knot pressed against Melody's neck and then stepped back.

'Any last words?' he asked callously.

Melody looked down at Dordoff standing on the ground before him. 'See you in hell, Frank.'

22

Sheriff Dordoff laughed mockingly. 'Don't hold your breath, J. T. I ain't planning on cashing in for — ' He broke off as a horse came galloping up to the closed gate. It slid to a stop and someone dismounted and pounded on the gate.

'Open up!' a man's voice bellowed.

Melody and everyone else turned toward the gate.

'Who is it?' Dordoff demanded.

'Marshal Ezra Macahan! Now open the damned gate, sheriff!'

Melody's pulse quickened.

Dordoff nodded to the deputies. One of them slid back the bolt and opened half of the gate.

Macahan, his black hat, black suit, white shirt and black string tie covered with trail dust, led his sweat-caked horse into the compound. The horse was almost as famous as the veteran lawman. A red dun, with a black dorsal stripe running from its tail to the crest of its head between its ears, it was unapproachable by anyone but the marshal, whom it followed like an obedient puppy.

A big man with naturally wide sloping shoulders, Macahan walked on the balls of his feet, Indian-style, slightly leaned forward as if eager to get to his destination. His craggy face was tanned and leathery from a life in the sun, his temples were gray and there was hardness to his pebble-gray eyes that only a glint of integrity saved from looking mean.

'What brings you here, Ezra?' Dordoff asked as the marshal confronted him.

'That's Marshal Macahan to you,' Macahan said curtly.

Dordoff flinched as if slapped and reddened.

'I'm here,' Macahan continued, 'to make sure the man you're hanging is guilty.'

'I wouldn't be hanging him if he weren't,' Dordoff replied tersely.

'Good. Then you won't mind filling me in on the details.'

'Be happy to. I rode out to the cabin where Trask lived with my sister and their daughters and found him standing over their dead bodies, still holding the knife he killed them with.'

'He's lying, Ezra,' Melody said from the gallows. 'I never stabbed — '

'Hush now, J. T.' Macahan said quietly. 'I'll be getting to your side of the story all in good time.' He paused as outside the compound, there was the sound of a wagon approaching at breakneck speed. It was accompanied by shouts from the driver as he urged the team to run faster.

Everyone turned toward the half-open gate. The fast-approaching wagon was still a hundred yards away, but immediately one of the deputies guarding the gate said: 'It's Roy Haney, marshal. Damn fool, he's going to kill himself if he ain't careful.'

'Open the other gate,' Macahan said. 'Just in case he can't make it through.'

The deputy obeyed.

Macahan turned to the hangman, who hadn't moved since the U.S. Marshal's arrival. 'Remove the noose from the prisoner, Harv. We don't want that trap sprung accidentally should the wagon sideswipe it.'

The hangman lifted the noose over Melody's head and stepped back from the trapdoor.

Melody also stepped back and grinned at Dordoff. 'Sorry to spoil your fun, Frank.'

'There'll be another day,' Dordoff said. 'Believe me, I'll watch you dance yet.'

The wagon and team were rapidly approaching the gate. The driver, a small thin man with red chin whiskers hanging over his farmer's coveralls, now saw Macahan and the others standing inside the compound and started yelling at them to wait!

Macahan removed his flat-crowned black hat and waved it at Haney, signaling for him to slow down.

Haney pulled back on the traces, trying to rein in the team. But the two foam-flecked horses had the bits between their teeth and were still running hard when they came busting in through the gate.

Everyone but Macahan scattered. As if immune to danger, the legendary lawman stood his ground, tall and straight-backed, defiantly daring the horses to run over him. For a moment it looked like they might oblige him. Then at the last instant they veered to the left, narrowly missing Macahan, dug their hooves in and came to a sliding, stiff-legged stop in front of the gallows. Dust swirled around them, almost hiding Melody and the hangman from sight.

'You damn old fool,' Macahan chided Haney. 'You trying to kill y'self and us along with you?'

'S-S-Sorry, m-m-marshal,' Haney

wheezed. 'But I didn't have no choice. Not if I wanted to save this fella's life.' He turned to Melody, adding: 'Looks like I didn't get here none too soon, J. T.'

'For which I'll always be grateful, Mr. Haney.'

'What the hell you going on about, old timer?' Dordoff barked at Haney. 'What's you being here got to do with whether J. T. hangs or not?'

'Catch your breath first, Roy,' Macahan said. 'Plenty of time left for a hanging.'

Haney took several deep breaths, exhaling loudly each time, and then, calmer now, said: 'I saw 'em, Ezra. I truly did. They didn't see me 'cause I was up in the loft, hidden behind the hay, but I saw them all right, yessir, saw 'em good, saw what they was doing too — '

'Saw who?' Macahan said patiently. 'Who'd you see, Roy?'

'Border trash! Drifters!'

'Drifters?' echoed Dordoff. 'That's

what this ruckus is all about? *Drifters?*'

'These drifters,' Melody said, curious, 'were there three of 'em by any chance?'

'Yeah, yeah,' Haney replied. 'Mean looking yahoos, too. But they didn't see me. No, sir, they never knew I was watching while they — the two of 'em held her down while this other fella, he took his own sweet time carving her up. Swear to God and never go to heaven, if I ain't telling the truth!'

'Makes sense,' Melody told Macahan. 'Most likely they're the same three drifters I saw coming from my place. Bastards! It never dawned on me then, but they must've just gotten through with . . . with my wife and the girls in our barn.'

'How convenient,' Dordoff sneered.

'Convenient?'

'Nothing like jumping on the band wagon, J. T. I suppose if the circus was in town you'd be blaming the clowns for your dirty work?'

'Not until I had the pleasure of

breaking your goddamn neck!' Melody growled.

Alarmed, Dordoff quickly stepped back beside Macahan.

'Easy now,' Macahan warned Melody. 'This ain't no time to be adding to your troubles.'

'It is understandable that he is angry,' Haney said. 'To be wrongfully accused of murdering the woman you love most — and your daughters too — I think maybe I would want to shoot this man myself.' He glared at Dordoff, who avoided eye contact with everyone.

'Let's get back to these drifters,' Macahan said to Haney. 'You actually saw them violating your housekeeper?'

'Yes, yes, in my barn. Poor Eva. Ever since I lose my beloved Helen, she has been of great comfort to me. And now, just when she needs me most, I cannot help her, cannot stop these men from doing bad things to her. What is worse, while they are doing these bad things they make jokes about . . . '

''Bout what, Roy?' Macahan said as

Haney stopped. 'What was it they were joking about?'

'How my Eva wasn't as much fun as . . . as . . . ' He paused, tears in his eyes as he looked sadly at Melody and said: 'Truly, I do not want to say this, my friend, because I too was once a father and I know how much pain it will bring, but — '

'It's all right, Roy. Go ahead,' Melody said, blood roaring in his ears. 'Never mind 'bout me. Just tell the marshal what it is you heard.'

'These bad men, they say they enjoy raping and stabbing your girls more than my Eva, 'cause they screamed louder and — '

'Okay, Roy,' Macahan interrupted. 'That's enough for now. I'll get the rest of the details later, when I take your statement. You all right?' he said, turning to Melody. 'Would you like a snort? I got a bottle of Old Hickory in my saddlebag.'

'Thanks, I'm fine, Ez.' Melody turned and faced Dordoff. 'Satisfied,

Frank? Or are you still convinced I'm guilty?'

Dordoff cleared his throat and tried to maintain what little dignity the star on his shirt brought him.

'Deputy,' he told Fisk. 'Remove your wrist-irons from this man.'

'Gladly,' Deputy Fisk said. Then to Melody: 'Turn around, J. T.'

Once the irons were removed, Melody massaged his wrists and gave the gallows a long look. As he did, he absently stroked his neck where the noose had been and then turned to Macahan and ruefully shook his head.

'That was too close for comfort, Ez.'

'Consider it a warning, *amigo*.'

'Warning?'

'Next time you're ready to draw down on a fella or do something that ain't legal, think 'bout the hangman's knot pressing against your neck . . . and walk away.'

'Good advice,' Melody said.

'You'll follow it?'

'Sure,' Melody said. 'First, though, I

got me three drifters to hunt down.'

'Which way were they headed when you last saw 'em?' Macahan said.

'West. New Mexico or Arizona, most likely.'

'I got business in Silverton. Feel like company?'

Melody grinned. 'Thought you'd never ask.'

23

The trail back toward Silverton was studded with countless hoof prints and wagon ruts. Hoping that the three horses ridden by the drifters had made some of the prints, Melody and Macahan rode at an easy, mile-consuming lope and by nightfall were less than two days' ride from town.

Making camp near a stand of giant Saguaro cactuses, they built a fire, spread their bedrolls and ate their hardtack and jerky while waiting for the coffee to boil.

'I been thinking,' Macahan said as he rolled himself a smoke. 'My business in Silverton could wait a few days. Maybe I'll tag along with you after these drifters.'

Melody smirked. 'To make sure they're guilty 'fore I gun them down?'

'To make sure they don't gun *you*

down 'fore you get the chance to find out.'

'Thanks for the vote of confidence.'

'Three against one is poor odds even for a fast gun like you.'

'True,' Melody agreed. 'And I'm happy to have your company. But I'm warning you, Ez. Don't try to stop me from killing these bastards if it turns out they're the ones who butchered Meryl and the girls. 'Cause by then, I won't be in the mood to listen to anyone. Not even you.'

'Before we work up a sweat 'bout that,' Macahan said patiently, 'let's first find out if they're the guilty ones.'

'Don't worry. I intend to do just that.' Melody filled two mugs with hot coffee and gave one to Macahan.

The marshal took a sip and grimaced. ''Course,' he said, 'it may all be moot.'

'How's that?'

'Depends on if we're still alive after drinking this black mud you call coffee — ' He broke off as in the nearby darkness a twig snapped underfoot, and then motioned to Melody that someone was out there.

Melody nodded to show he'd heard it too and quietly drew his Colt.

'Hey, the camp . . . ' a voice called out. 'Don't shoot. I'm coming in.'

'Come ahead,' Macahan said. 'But move nice and easy, ma'am . . . and keep your hands away from your guns.'

Melody looked at Macahan and mouthed: 'Ain't that Liberty?'

Macahan shrugged. 'Sounds like. But we're too far south for it to be her . . . '

Both men waited as footsteps crunched through the dead cactus spines, followed by the heavier sound of a horse plodding along after its owner.

Suddenly a shadowy figure appeared out of the darkness, leading a sweating blue roan stallion. At first glance it could have been a man. But a second look left no doubt that it was an attractive, strong-featured woman in her late twenties. Tall and lean, she wore a doeskin jacket over a plaid shirt and jeans and strands of sun-streaked brown hair poked out from under the brim of her soiled campaign hat. Holstered on her hip was a Colt .45, and a Winchester Model '86 protruded from under her saddle.

'I thought that was you,' Deputy U.S. Marshal Liberty Mercer said to Macahan. Then as she recognized Melody: 'I'll be damned. J. T.! Mite far out of your territory, ain't you?'

'No more than you,' he said.

'True,' she admitted. 'But to arrest the sonsofbitches I'm tracking, I'll ride to Hades itself if necessary. Boy,' she added, squatting by the fire, 'that coffee sure smells delicious.'

'Better than it tastes,' Macahan said, 'that's for damn sure.'

'Help yourself,' Melody told Liberty. 'It's my special brew. It's just that 'certain folks,'' he added, glaring Macahan, 'don't appreciate good taste.'

'After riding as far as I have,' Liberty said, going to her horse and taking a tin mug from her saddlebag, 'it could taste like mud for all I care.'

'Be careful what you wish for,' Macahan murmured.

Leaving one glove on, Liberty grabbed the hot coffee pot, filled her mug and returned the pot to the flames. She then gulped down a mouthful of coffee. For an instant she didn't react. Then her eyebrows arched and grimacing, she exclaimed: 'Urgh! What was it I was saying about mud?'

Macahan stifled a chuckle.

'Hey, nobody's forcing you to drink it,' grumbled Melody.

'True, true,' Liberty said, 'and under the circumstances, I hate to complain, but . . . ' She took another swallow and grimaced again. 'All I hope, J. T. is that you got a license to brew this — whatever it is, 'cause, sure as hell, it's going to seriously deplete the male population.'

'Why do you think he's keeps *me* around?' Macahan deadpanned.

'To save him from getting shot by all

the angry widows would be my guess,' Liberty said.

'Go ahead,' Melody said as they both laughed, 'make jokes, laugh your fool heads off for all I care. I'm going to have the last laugh when I open my trading post and become famous for my coffee.'

'Trading post, you say?' Liberty hid a wink to Macahan before adding: 'Funny you should mention that, J. T. I knew this Indian agent once. Odd bird, named Lon McKay. Had himself a trading post in the Black Hills. This was back in '76, right before that damn fool Custer got himself slaughtered up on the Little Big Horn.'

Macahan rolled his eyes in mock despair. 'Dear God, not that old saw again.'

'Most of the hostiles were on the reservation at the time,' Liberty continued as if Macahn hadn't spoken, 'and things were right peaceful. Well, one night this old chief named Blue Tongue, who was Sitting Bull's cousin, slips off the res' and steals some firewater. Next thing you know he's drunker than six hoot owls and collapses outside the trading post. Now McKay, he doesn't want any trouble, so he tries to sober him up with black coffee. Suddenly, after 'bout ten cups of the stuff, ol' Blue Tongue, he gets a bellyache to end all bellyaches and jumps up, hollering and dancing around like he's doing a war dance. Next thing you know — '

'Don't tell me,' Melody said sourly, 'Sitting Bull thinks his cousin has been poisoned, rounds up the Sioux and massacres Custer and the 7th Cavalry in revenge?'

Liberty pretended to be suspicious as she stared at Melody. 'Have I told you this story before?'

'No more than a hundred times.'

'A thousand would be more like it,' Macahan said.

'Really? Ah, well,' Liberty said, resigned. 'Reckon it's time I came up with a new story.'

'Either that,' Macahan said, 'or find

new victims to lie to.'

They all broke out laughing.

Macahan then threw his coffee dregs into the fire, making it sizzle, and turned to Liberty. 'These jaspers you're tracking? They must've really stirred the pot for you to have followed them all the way from Guthrie?'

'Damn right they did. Sonsofbitches slaughtered three families that we know of and there could be more.'

'Where'd this happen?' asked Melody.

'The first two were in Indian Territory and the last one was just this side of the border.'

'So you reckon they're making their way south?'

'Seems like. No-good bastards,' she said angrily. 'They gut-shot the men folk so they'd die real slow and painful, then raped and butchered the women like so much raw meat. On top of that, what really makes me sick is, four of the victims were girls, no more than eleven or twelve — '

'Whoa,' Melody said, interrupting.

'These men — are they drifters?'

'Yeah.'

'How many are there?' put in Macahan. 'Three, maybe?'

'Uh-uh. Four that I know of, maybe more. Why?'

'J. T. is after three drifters that raped and stabbed his wife and girls to death.'

'Oh dear God,' Liberty breathed. She fondly squeezed Melody's shoulder. 'I'm so sorry to hear that, J. T. What a dreadful thing to happen.'

He nodded his thanks, and said grimly: 'You can see why this is kind of personal with me?'

'Hell, yes,' Liberty said. 'Damn their stinking hides!'

'One thing's for certain,' Melody said. 'When I do catch up with them, and believe me I *will* catch up to them, no matter how long it takes, I'll make sure they regret the day they were ever born!'

He spat chaw juice into the crackling of the flames.

'You know,' Liberty said after a

pause, 'all the time I've been dogging these lice I've been asking myself how anyone could be capable of committing such a vicious inhuman act — especially against helpless innocent young girls.'

'That's a question only the Man upstairs can answer,' Macahan said.

'If there *is* a Man upstairs,' Melody said bitterly. 'Which I'm seriously starting to doubt.'

'"Who never doubted never half believed,"' Macahan quoted, thinking aloud.

If Melody heard him, he didn't show it. He sat still as a stone, gazing fixedly into the flames dancing before him, his eyes burning with intense rage and hatred.

'Could be,' he said presently.

'Could be what?' asked Macahan.

'They're one and the same.'

'Your drifters and mine, you mean?' put in Liberty.

'All I'm saying is,' Melody said, 'it'd be a sorry day in hell if there was *two* groups, both unrelated, both committing murder and debauchery at once.'

It was such a sobering thought no one felt like responding.

After a little, Macahan got up and stretched the stiffness from his back. 'You're welcome to spread your roll with us,' he told Liberty. 'Though I'll understand if you feel a need to keep after these lousy butchers.'

'*Gracias*,' she said. 'My roan is pure wore out, so reckon I'll take you up on your offer. If that's okay with you, J. T.?'

Melody didn't answer. He sat, motionless, staring into the fire. In his imagination he saw the faces of his wife and daughters in the flames. All three were smiling.

He smiled back.

His daughters giggled and both blew him a kiss.

He went to blow a kiss back to them.

But just then a breeze blew in off the desert, fanning the flames, sending sparks flying, and when the flames returned to normal the faces had disappeared.

It was the saddest moment of his life.

24

They skipped breakfast the next morning so they could get an early start. Melody boiled a pot of coffee but other than himself, there were no takers. The three of them mounted up and pulled on their slickers to shield them from the heavy dawn dew.

The sun hadn't come up yet. But a sliver of moon glimmered in the dark sky and by its silvery light they followed the trail leading to Silverton. They made good time, stopping only to give the horses a breather, and were less than a day's ride from town when Melody noticed how some of the hoof prints had veered off to the west.

Telling Macahan and Liberty to hold up, he dismounted, hunkered down and counted the prints. 'I make it seven — possibly eight riders altogether.'

'You figure it's them?' Macahan asked.

'I've no idea, Ez. I wouldn't know their tracks from any other, but . . . '

'But what?' Liberty questioned.

'It's just a gut feeling I got,' Melody said. 'But, yeah, I think it's them.'

'But you said you saw three drifters,' Macahan reminded. 'Not seven.'

'I know. But Liberty said she was trailing four or five men. Correct?' he asked her.

She nodded, saying: 'In other words, you think this is where they joined up?'

Melody shrugged. 'Like I said, it's just a gut feeling.'

'And you're going to follow it?' Macahan said.

'I know it's *loco*,' Melody admitted, 'but . . . yeah, I am. But that's no reason why you two should. I mean, I'd hate to have you ride miles out of your way only to find out it's not them.'

Macahan traded looks with Liberty and though neither said a word, the marshal turned to Melody and nodded to show he could count on them.

Melody grinned, relieved, but knew better than to thank them. Friends as close as they were needed no thanks; in fact any sign of gratitude only embarrassed them. And that was the last thing he wanted to do. So, he swung up into the saddle and the three of them rode west in the direction of a range of low craggy hills.

'What do you reckon their plan is?' Macahan said as they loped along.

'I don't know,' Liberty answered. 'Truthfully, I'd be happy just to know where the bastards are headed. I mean other than Silverton, which we're riding away from, there's no town within miles of here.'

'No, but there are plenty of mines,' reminded Melody. 'Especially in those hills.'

Liberty and Macahan looked at him in surprise.

'What're you saying, J.T?' the marshal asked. 'That they're going to steal the ore from the miners?'

'Nope. I ain't saying that at all. But what I *am* saying is, if my theory is right, they're going to hide out in the hills somewhere near the trail leading to the mines, and then when the payroll from the bank in Silverton — '

' — *heavily-guarded* payroll,' corrected Macahan.

' — is delivered by pack-train to the miners — '

' — the drifters, now turned bandits, will rob it before it reaches the mines — '

' — and then ride like hell for the border before a posse catches them,' Melody said.

'Not a bad plan,' Liberty said.

'Matter of fact, it's a damned good one,' said Macahan. 'The bank pays the miners in silver dollars.'

'Thousands upon thousands upon thousands of beautiful, shiny, silver dollars!' concluded Melody. 'Easily spent and all untraceable!'

Liberty's eyebrows arched in appreciation of the amount.

'Now that's just a guess,' Melody continued. 'But considering the direction the drifters are headed and based on what a certain lady friend told me about the Silver Train and how punctual it is, not to mention what I know about the town marshal and the manager of the bank — who also happens to be the lady's father — well, it wouldn't surprise me if I was right on target.'

'Lady friend?' Liberty said suspiciously. 'What lady friend? And don't give me that smirk, J. T., because I've heard all about your conquests even as far away as little ol' Guthrie, Oklahoma!'

'What have you heard?' Melody said.

'That tough as you are, and as fast with a gun as you are, you're something of a soft touch when it comes to the ladies.'

'Gullible is the word that comes to mind,' Macahan said wryly.

'As in: easily twisted around their little finger,' explained Liberty.

'Well, you've heard wrong,' Melody said, irked. 'Both of you. Do I like women? Course I do. What man doesn't? But as for being gullible or easily seduced, well, it just ain't true.'

'I'm glad to hear that,' Macahan said drily. 'Perhaps, under the circumstances, you would be willing to share what exactly this 'lady friend' and Marshal Garrett divulged to you? You know: In the interest of justice?'

'Gladly,' said Melody. Slowing his horse to a walk, he waited until they were alongside him and then revealed everything he knew about Theodore Avery and Tom Garrett, including their criminal activities.

'And the way you left it,' Macahan said, 'Garrett thinks you're going to step in and take his place?'

'Yup.'

'What about these drifters?' asked Liberty. 'Where do you think they fit in all of this?'

'Nowhere,' Melody said. 'I could be wrong but I don't think they're connected to Garrett.'

'Mean there being here at the same time is just a coincidence?'

'That'd be my guess.'

'I don't believe in coincidences,' Macahan said.

'Me neither,' Liberty added.

Melody shrugged. 'Ordinarily I'd agree with both of you. But in this case . . . ' He shrugged again, adding: 'It's possible, of course, that they're part of Garrett's crew. But I very much doubt that. Because as the Foley brothers discovered while they were part of the posse, Garrett's way of getting rid of any competition or people that might cause him problems, is a bullet in the back.'

'What's to prevent him doing the same to you?' Liberty said.

'Nothing, except I honestly believe he wants to free himself of this mess and retire to his spread near Tucson. And if that's true, he needs me as his replacement, which means it ain't in his best interest to shoot me.'

'And if you're wrong?' Macahan said.

'I'll deal with Garrett if and when it's necessary. Right now, though, the only thing that matters is tracking these drifters down and weeding out the three that . . . murdered Meryl and the girls.'

25

They rode three abreast at an easy lope, and after a half-hour or so, off to the east, the sun began inching above the distant mountain peaks. Liberty stared at the golden orb as if it were an old friend.

'You know,' she said wistfully, 'it's too bad my father isn't here to back our play. He lives for this sort of bravado.'

'He'd be mighty welcome,' said Melody, 'that's for sure.'

'Speaking of your pa,' Macahan said, 'how is Drifter?'

'Fine — I reckon.'

'Where is he, do you know?'

'Your guess is as good as mine,' Liberty replied. 'Last I heard he was in Santa Rosa, but that's been — oh, what — three or four months. Maybe longer. And before that, Mexico, I think.' She chuckled ruefully. 'Keeping track of my father is a full-time job in itself — a job, I might add, I gave up long ago. I mean much as I love him — and he loves me — the plain and simple truth is, some men aren't cut out to be fathers and my dad's one of them.' She smiled sadly, her voice full of regret as she said: 'Of course it should've come as no surprise. After all, he isn't called Drifter for nothing.'

'That's true,' agreed Melody. 'But I'll tell you this, Liberty, a better man doesn't exist.'

'I couldn't agree more,' Macahan said. 'And you're right when you say he loves you, Emily, 'cause if he's told me once he's told me a hundred times that the luckiest day of his life was when he discovered you were his daughter.'

Liberty gave a little laugh, as if she neither believed nor disbelieved the marshal.

'What?' Macahan said. 'Did I say something funny?'

'No, I was just thinking,' she said. 'You and my dad, you're the only people who ever call me by my real name.'

'If it offends you, Emily, I won't call you it again.'

'Offends? Oh, my goodness no. Quite the opposite. It makes me feel all warm inside, you know, as if I was part of something, a family who loves m-me.' She choked on the last few words and tears flooded her eyes. 'Dammit,' she exclaimed. 'Damn, damn, dammit. What the hell's the matter with me? If this keeps up, next I'll be singing nursery rhymes!' She dug her spurs into the roan, startling it into a gallop and quickly pulled her ahead of them.

Macahan looked at Melody and regretfully shook his head. 'I don't know any man I admire or respect more than Drifter, but by God I wish he'd realize what his drifting is doing to his daughter.'

'Have you ever talked to him about it?'

'No, and I don't intend to,' Macahan said firmly. 'Thanks to this job, I stick my damn nose in enough different lives without adding one of my friends to the list.'

'Couldn't you justify it by thinking of how much good it might do Liberty?' Melody said. 'When you consider everything she's been through it wouldn't hurt to give her a little help. Hell, I'd do it myself 'cept I don't know him as well as you do.'

Macahan didn't answer. His gaze was fixed on Liberty, who, having regained control of her emotions, had reined in her blue roan some fifty yards ahead and was now waiting for them to catch up.

'Don't get me wrong,' Melody continued. 'I'm not trying to tell you what to do, Ez. You know me well enough to know I'd never do that. But Liberty's good people, too, and deserves maybe a little more attention than she's getting from Drifter.'

Again Macahan didn't answer. He was silent for so long Melody wondered if he'd heard him. It was then, far off, a lonely coyote yip-yipped to the pale fading moon. The sound seemed to bring Macahan to life. Releasing his frustration in a long, drawn-out sigh, he said: 'You're right, *amigo*. Emily does deserve better. A whole lot better.'

'So you'll talk to him?' Melody said.

Macahan nodded. 'If the opportunity ever arises, and he's in the right mood, I'll give it a try. That's the best I can promise you, J. T.'

'That's good enough for me,' Melody said. 'Now, let's go find those goddamn drifters. It's time we made them suffer for all the pain they've caused so many others.'

'I'm with you there,' Macahan said.

Both men kicked up their horses and galloped toward Liberty, who, having regained her poise, sat proudly on her stallion with a brave, tight-lipped smile on her chiseled face.

26

The hoof prints made by the seven or eight riders led Melody, Macahan and Liberty deep into the craggy hills that had once been rich with silver ore. Years of mining had robbed them of much of their natural treasure, but they still yielded sufficient ore to make it worthwhile for the Atherton Mining Company to keep the mines open.

But the veins of silver were now harder to find. And miners had to dig dangerously deep under the hills to find them and then work longer hours in order to produce enough ore to make the whole operation profitable. Cave-ins were frequent and at that depth almost always fatal for the trapped workers. Aware of this, AMC induced men to work for them by paying double the normal wage and promising to take care of the families of any miners who were killed while working in the mines.

Melody, Macahan and Liberty followed the hoof prints along the main trail as it climbed past the entrances of the numerous mine-shafts. Many of them were no longer in use. But the ones that were buzzed with activity as workers transferred the extracted ore from the mine carts to mule-drawn wagons, which then carried the ore downhill and across the scrubland to Silverton. Armed guards stood watching each loading procedure, while others on horseback escorted each wagon downhill to a dry creek-bed that snaked between the hills. There, at the entrance to the hills, the ore-wagons joined an already awaiting wagon train that was guarded by more mounted guards waiting to escort them to Silverton.

By now the sun had cleared the mountains and its warm brightness yellowed the hillsides and turned the coat of Liberty's blue roan an eye-catching silvery gray. There was no sign of the riders other than the hoof prints, which were getting harder to find among the countless mule tracks and ruts caused by the wheels of the ore-wagons.

'Where the hell are these yahoos headed to?' Melody growled. 'I've hidden in these hills enough times to know there's nothing ahead but more of the same.'

'Beats me,' Macahan said. 'But keep your eyes peeled. I doubt if the bastards know we're dogging their trail, but it never hurts to be on the safe side.'

'Yeah, and besides,' Melody said, reining up as the prints were lost among other tracks, 'maybe some of the workers are being paid to act as lookouts so they can warn the drifters when lawmen are coming. I ain't saying it's so,' he added as Liberty gave him a dubious look, 'but you got to admit it's possible.'

'But unlikely,' she replied. 'These men are paid handsomely and on a regular basis. That's a winning combination and a man would have to be a damned fool to risk a steady income for the chance to steal a few silver dollars.'

'It's more than a few,' Melody said. 'There are a lot of miners working up here, most if not all employed by AMC. That translates into thousands of dollars.'

'He's right,' agreed Macahan. 'And don't forget, they don't have to risk cave-ins or lunger's disease to get their hands on the money, either.'

'No, just bullets,' Liberty said grimly. 'Which might be a kinder, quicker death, but it's still death just the same and I — ' She broke off, startled, as a huge explosion rocked the hills.

The thunderous detonation came from a large mine on the opposite hillside, and even as her roan and the horses of Melody and Macahan all reared up in terror, flames and smoke came belching out of the entrance.

When the smoke cleared, the entrance had collapsed, trapping the miners working inside behind a wall of rock.

At once the men working in the other mines poured out of the entrances, picks and shovels in hand, the candles in their head-lamps still burning, their faces all expressing the same emotion: fear, not for themselves but for their buried fellow-workers.

En masse they stopped working and rushed down the various slopes to the bottom of each hill, across the dry creek-bed and on, scrambling up the opposite hillside. They weren't alone. The guards and drivers of the ore-wagons followed them, leaving the wagons in the riverbed unprotected.

'C'mon,' Liberty told Macahan and Melody, 'we've got to help them.'

'Whoa, hang on,' Macahan said. 'At the risk of sounding callous, that's exactly what they want us to do.'

'They?' said Melody.

Macahan thumbed at the riders who'd just come galloping out of the entrance of an abandoned mine close to the ore-wagon train. Bandannas hid their faces but there was no mistaking their horses or the number of riders: seven!

'Those bastards!' Liberty exclaimed as five of the drifters dismounted, turned their horses over to their two cohorts and jumped onto the wagons. 'They must've doubled back and planted those charges, knowing the cave-in would act as a diversion.'

'Yeah,' said Macahan. 'Sonsofbitches outsmarted us!'

'At the cost of those miners' lives!' growled Liberty.

'Which means I was wrong all along,' said Melody. 'They weren't after the payroll. They're going to rob the Silver Train!'

'Wrong again,' Liberty said. 'My guess is they're not after the ore at all. They're going to rob the bank that *pays* the payroll!'

'You could be right,' agreed Macahan. 'The Pinks are going to see those familiar wagons and even though they won't recognize the drivers, for a moment they're going to be confused and in that moment, the drifters will gun 'em down and rob the bank!'

'Then what're we waiting for?' Melody said, whirling his horse around. 'Let's ruin their party!' He spurred his dark-maned bay down the hillside, quickly followed by Macahan and Liberty.

27

The drivers of the ore-wagons whipped the mules into a gallop and raced across the flatland toward Silverton. They were escorted by the two drifters on horseback, who were leading the drivers' saddled horses.

None of the miners or guards noticed the wagons leaving; they were all too busy frantically digging at the rocks blocking the entrance to the caved-in mine.

Riding at a reckless pace Melody led Macahan and Liberty down the steep hillside, loose dirt cascading after them. They soon reached the arroyo at the bottom. After eons of no water the dry creek-bed was rock-hard, enabling them to spur their horses into a full-out run. They soon began to catch up with the mule-drawn ore-wagons.

One of the mounted drifters, fearful

of pursuit, looked back and saw them coming. He yelled at the drivers to whip more speed out of the teams, then he and the other rider dismounted and took cover behind some rocks. From here they opened fire at Melody and his companions, hoping to drive them back. Their first volley hit nothing, but the second killed Macahan's famous red dun. It went down in a heap, throwing the veteran marshal over its head. He landed hard and went sprawling.

Melody and Liberty reined up, dismounted, dropped to one knee and returned fire. Melody's bullets ricocheted off the rock near the first drifter's head, forcing him to duck for cover.

Liberty was even more accurate. Her third round put a hole in the second drifter's forehead and he collapsed without a sound.

Macahan, Winchester in hand, came limping up behind Melody and Liberty, barking: 'Go after those damn' wagons while I cover you.'

Obeying, they quickly mounted and spurred away, while the marshal opened fire at the first drifter, keeping him pinned behind the rock.

Melody and Liberty rode straight at the first drifter and as they galloped past him, both emptied their Colts into him. He slumped against the rock, dead.

'Go after them,' Liberty told Melody, 'while I pick up Ezra.' Without waiting for his answer, she whirled her blue roan around and raced back toward Macahan.

Melody galloped after the ore-wagons. He soon closed in on them and pulling his Winchester, fired at the driver of the nearest wagon. It took three shots but the fourth round knocked the driver from the seat. He fell forward, between the two galloping mules, and was run over by one of the rear wheels. The mules immediately slowed down, reins trailing between them, and within moments Melody over-took the slow-moving wagon.

Glancing at the driver to make sure he was dead, Melody then galloped on after the other four wagons.

The drivers whipped their teams harder, but the laboring mules had nothing left and Melody soon caught up to them. He fired his last two rounds at the driver handling the slowest of the teams. The driver dropped the reins and fell off the wagon, dead before he hit the ground.

Melody raced on after the remaining wagons. As he rode he reloaded his rifle, guiding the galloping bay with his knees. Suddenly shots came from behind him. For an instant he thought it was the driver he'd thought was dead that was firing at him. But when he looked back, he saw it was Macahan, riding double behind Liberty, who was doing the shooting.

The marshal's bullets killed one of the three remaining drivers. He slumped forward, reins slipping from his lifeless fingers, and fell from the wagon-box. The mules veered to their left, dragging the off-balanced wagon sideways. One of its wheels hit a rock, bouncing the wagon into the air. When it landed the rear axle broke and the wagon over-turned, sending ore flying everywhere.

The two remaining drivers, realizing they couldn't outrun Melody or Liberty and Macahan, pulled up the exhausted mules and raised their hands in surrender.

Melody drew level with them, reined up and covered them with his Winchester. 'Throw down your guns,' he ordered, 'and get off those wagons.'

Grudgingly, they obeyed him.

Melody studied their faces, hoping that they were two of the three drifters whom he believed had raped and murdered his wife and daughters. They weren't. He'd never seen these men before. Disappointed, he turned to greet Liberty and Macahan as they rode up.

'It ain't them,' he said bitterly to Macahan.

Knowing how crushed he must feel,

Macahan said encouragingly: 'Don't worry, J. T. They'll show up one day, most likely when you least expect it.'

Melody nodded. 'Till then,' he said grimly, 'nothing else matters.'

'These the fellas you've been hunting?' Macahan asked Liberty.

She nodded. 'Two of them, anyway. The other two have already bit the bullet back there.' She nodded in the direction of the other dead drifters.

'Reckon the sensible thing for us to do now,' Macahan said, 'is take the prisoners to Silverton and lock 'em up till they go before a judge.'

Liberty nodded. 'If it's okay with you, marshal, I'd like to stick around to hear His Honor sentence them to hang.'

'What for we going to hang?' demanded one of the drifters. 'We ain't done nothing to earn us a rope.'

'You call raping and murdering whole families nothing?' Liberty said to them.

'We never raped nor murdered

nobody,' the other drifter protested. 'All we done is robbed two Overland stages and shot a gambler in Abilene who was dealing seconds.'

'That's the truth,' said the other drifter, 'swear to God, marshal.'

'Don't plead your case to me,' Liberty told them. 'Save that for the judge and jury.'

'Get up on those wagon boxes,' Macahan ordered the drifters. 'You were so all-fire anxious to reach Silverton, now you're going to get your wish.'

28

It was mid-morning when they rode into town and escorted the drifters into the marshal's office.

Garrett was at his desk, feet up, cleaning his Winchester. He looked up as they entered and greeted them curtly. He waited until Liberty had removed her wrist-irons from the prisoners, and then told Deputy Fisk to put both men in one of the cells.

Melody watched the lawman's face when he first saw the prisoners, hoping that Garrett would react in some way that suggested he either knew the drifters or was somehow involved in the failed robbery. But Garrett's expression never changed and neither of the drifters showed any sign of recognition, adding to Melody's overall disappointment.

Sensing how low he felt, Macahan

asked Melody and Liberty to accompany him to the bank. 'I want to talk to the manager,' he explained, 'and get his reaction to what happened. I don't know if he's involved in this or not, but I got some questions that need answering and I don't want it to sound like I'm interrogating him. So since you,' he said to Melody, 'know him — '

' — *and* his daughter,' Liberty needled. 'Let's not forget her, the little darlin'.'

Macahan ignored her. ' — maybe he'd feel more comfortable if the questions came from you.'

'He might,' admitted Melody. ' — 'specially if Garrett's already told him 'bout me becoming his new partner in crime.'

'Well, either way it can't hurt,' Macahan said. He gingerly rubbed his left shoulder which had been bruised when his horse was shot out from under him, before adding: 'Only thing that matters is we find out who's behind all this and if, like you thought, these seven drifters just 'coincidently' happened to get involved or were part of Avery's grand scheme from the git-go.'

'My guess is that Avery's up to his neck in this,' Melody said. 'But having been wrong before, I'm going to keep my opinion to myself and wait and see how things turn out.'

'In other words,' Liberty teased, '"once bitten, twice shy.' That it, Romeo?'

'All right, all right,' Macahan grumbled before Melody could respond, 'rein your humor in, Emily. I got enough things to worry about. I don't need to listen to you two bickering like a couple of old married bush hens!'

★ ★ ★

Avery, on seeing the three of them enter the bank, came bustling out of his office to meet them. Melody sensed his boisterous, effervescent greeting was strictly for their benefit and wondered whether inside Avery was shaking in his boots. If he was, he hid it behind a big welcoming smile that showed no trace of nervousness.

Inviting them into his office, he waited until they were seated and then asked Macahan how he could be of service to them.

'I'll let Deputy Trask answer that, sir,' Macahan replied congenially. 'He's running this show. Marshal Mercer and I, we're just passengers 'long for the ride.'

Melody wasn't sure but thought he noticed relief enter Avery's eyes. It was gone almost instantly, followed by genuine surprise as Avery said: '*Deputy Trask?* Why, I had no idea you were a lawman, young fella?'

'I deputized him,' Macahan said before Melody could answer. 'I figured three against seven was better than two. Especially since these men had committed a number of exceptionally vicious crimes.'

'I see,' Avery said cautiously. 'Yes, yes, of course, you were quite right to do so.' He beamed at Melody. 'You may not know it, marshal, but this man is something of a hero. He saved my daughter's life and as a result, I am eternally grateful to him.'

'I fished her out of a river,' Melody said quickly. 'Wasn't nothing heroic 'bout it. Just a matter of being in the right place at the right time.'

'Nevertheless,' Avery said, 'I'm indebted to you and hope I've made it clear that if there's anything I can ever do for you — '

'Matter of fact, there is,' Melody said. 'I was following these men 'cause I thought they were the ones who murdered my wife and daughters. Turns out they weren't, but since we believe they intended to rob your bank, I wondered if you would come over to the jail and see if you recognize them.'

Avery frowned, as if the idea was absurd. 'I can answer that question without going anywhere,' he said emphatically. 'I happened to be entering the bank when you brought them in and I can assure you that I've never seen either man before. Ever.'

'That's good to know,' Melody said. ''Cause when Marshal Mercer was putting them in irons, they hinted that someone at the bank was behind the intended robbery.'

His lie served its purpose: Avery nervously licked his lips.

'What 'intended robbery'?' he demanded. 'I thought these men were charged with stealing silver ore from the mines, and for being responsible for causing a cave-in that trapped the men digging inside?'

'Bad news travels fast around here,' Liberty remarked casually.

'Yeah, and apparently on the wings of invisible doves,' Macahan murmured.

Melody, thinking the same thing, said: 'They were, Mr. Avery. But the cave-in was a diversion so they could be free to come here and rob the bank. Oh, and while we're on the subject of the cave-in, sir, would you mind telling us who told you about it?'

'W-Why . . . uh . . . I don't remember exactly,' Avery stammered.

'Think,' Melody said firmly. 'It's important, sir.'

'Well, I . . . there were a crowd outside the bank when I walked up. Everyone was talking at once and I . . . I must have overheard someone mention it or . . . maybe even heard it from Marshal Garrett. He and I were talking just moments before the culprits were brought in and — '

'It wasn't the marshal, Mr. Avery,' Melody said, interrupting, 'or anyone you overheard on the street. They were as much in the dark as anyone.'

'W-Well, it had to be . . . s-someone,' Avery blustered. 'I mean how else would I have heard the news?'

'That's exactly my point,' Melody said bluntly. 'So how else do you think you heard about it?'

'Don't misunderstand, sir,' Macahan added as Avery looked trapped. 'We aren't suggesting that you personally were involved in this chicanery.'

'Absolutely not,' Liberty assured. 'It's the person who told you or you overheard that we're after. Because as I'm sure Deputy Trask was about to mention, the men we brought in, the men I removed my irons from, didn't have a chance to tell anyone what they'd done. We made sure of that by keeping them away from everyone.'

'Everyone 'cept Deputy Fisk and Marshal Garrett,' Melody reminded, as if offering Avery a way out.

'The marshal!' Avery exclaimed. 'Of course, that's who must've told me. Tom Garrett is not only a valued customer, he's a personal friend.'

'I'm sure he is,' Macahan said patiently. 'But, unfortunately, both he and Deputy Fisk were still in the marshal's office when we left. And since we came straight here, well, you can see that presents a bit of a conundrum.'

'Yes . . . well . . . then I've no idea who told me,' Avery said, his bluster now growing panicky. 'But obviously *someone* did or else I wouldn't know anything about it, now would I?'

'No,' Melody said. 'You wouldn't, sir.'

'Well, then, I'm sorry but I can't help you. And now that you know that,' Avery continued quickly, 'do you have any more questions? Because if you haven't, then I'm afraid I must ask you to leave. I'm terribly busy and — '

'There is one question,' Melody prodded gently. 'It concerns Marshal Garrett.'

'What about him?'

'Well, since you're a friend of his, maybe you can explain why he hired two gunmen to shoot me, men I had to kill before they could tell me themselves?'

For a fleeting moment Avery paled and sweat beaded on his forehead. Then he quickly recovered and said: 'You must be mistaken, Mr. Melody. The Marshal Garrett I know — and may I say, admire — would never stoop to such unsavory behavior. Knowing Tom as well as I do, I can guarantee you that other than the riff-raff he arrests, he has no connection with any gunmen. No connection whatsoever. Now,' he said, rising, 'if you'll excuse me, I really do have to get back to work. I have some important documents that need my signature and — '

'Of course,' Macahan said, rising along with Melody and Liberty. 'We won't take up any more of your time, sir.' He opened the door for Liberty, adding: 'Nice quiet little town you have here, Mr. Avery. I'd hate to see it destroyed on account of a botched up robbery.'

'Destroyed?'

'Yes, sir. Unless I get to the bottom of this and weed out exactly who masterminded it, that's exactly what'll happen when I notify the Federal Government and they send in the military.'

'W-What?' Avery looked panicky. 'Why would you want to do that, marshal?'

'Not a question of *wanting* to do anything, Mr. Avery. In instances like this, it's the law, which means I got no choice. See, you — or should I say the robbers are stealing silver that belongs to the Denver mint, which is owned by the Federal Govern — '

'But there hasn't *been* a robbery,' Avery said desperately.

'No,' put in Melody, 'but there was an attempted robbery and in the eyes of the folks running Washington, that's almost the same thing.'

'You know how politicians are, Mr. Avery,' said Liberty. 'Hell, they're all Union boys. And Union boys look at things entirely differently than we do out West. I mean, here we take a man at his word — '

'Exactly,' Macahan put in. 'But back in Washington, Mr. Avery, that ain't the case. These table-thumpers, they're looking for votes . . . issues that'll get them reelected . . . and once their mind is made up 'bout a fella, no matter who he is, all the sand in Arizona couldn't change their minds.'

There was silence as Avery wet his

lips and desperately searched for a way out.

'Marshal,' Melody said to Macahan, 'I wonder if I could have a few words with Mr. Avery — alone!'

'Sure thing, deputy.' Macahan nodded at Liberty and they left the office.

Melody closed the door behind them and faced Avery, who sat squirming behind his desk.

'I'm going to come right to the point, sir. By the way things are shaping up, I can tell Marshal Macahan feels he needs someone to take the blame for this. Knowing him like I do I doubt if he cares who it is, just so it's someone whose hide he can nail to the wall to get Washington off his neck.'

'W-What're you getting at?' Avery said, panicking. 'I'm not throwing myself to the wolves if that's what you think. And if you care about Regan, as much as I think you do, you won't ask me to.'

'Relax, Mr. Avery. I'm not suggesting anything of the sort.'

Avery sagged with relief.

'I know you're nothing but an innocent victim in all this. I also know how Marshal Garrett has been prodding you into helping him with all these robberies by threatening to expose you to your daughter — '

'Regan — what's she got to do with this?' blustered Avery.

'Come now, sir, this ain't the time for blowing smoke. We both know that you promised her mother you'd give Regan the kind of life she deserves. And we both know you'd love to honor that promise. But that takes money, Mr. Avery — money you didn't have — money that you had to embezzle from the bank — '

'Oh dear God,' Avery groaned. 'Is there anything you don't know about me?'

'I know that you'd give anything to get out from under Garrett's manipulating, greedy thumb,' Melody said. Then, before Avery could respond: 'And that's what I'm offering you, sir — a chance to do exactly that.'

'How?'

'By confessing everything illegal that you and Garrett are involved in.'

'B-But if I do that, I'll go to prison same as him.'

'You'll have to do some time, yeah. But I'm sure a smart lawyer can persuade the judge to be lenient with you when it comes time for sentencing. After all, without your evidence, they have nothing on Garrett. He's going to walk away free and retire to his spread. What's more, eventually you'll take all the blame when the Federal marshals end up pinning this on you. It's up to you, sir,' Melody added when Avery didn't respond. 'If you don't want to do this, don't. I won't tell them anything — I couldn't do that to Regan. She'd hate me for the rest of my life and that ain't something I'm prepared to live with.'

Before Avery could respond, Melody opened the door and signaled to Macahan and Liberty. Both entered the office. Then, as Melody and Liberty stood with their backs to the door,

Macahan leaned on the desk and looked Avery squarely in the eye.

'Well, sir,' he said, 'is there anything you want to tell me?'

Avery looked at Melody, at Macahan, then at Melody again. None of them blinked. Avery wet his lips, sighed heavily and nodded.

Macahan smiled and straightened up. 'Then let's get at it.'

Before Avery could start talking Melody opened the door and turned to Liberty, saying: 'Let's you and me go get some coffee. I know the perfect place.'

Liberty hesitated, sensing she was walking into a trap, and then walked out.

'We'll be across the street at McGee's,' Melody told Macahan. 'Little café that serves the worst coffee in the world.'

Macahan smiled. 'Revenge is a dish best served hot,' he quoted.

'Actually,' Melody said, ''cording to this Creole gal I knew in New Orleans, it's best served cold. But either way's fine with me.'

29

It was early afternoon and blazing hot by the time Avery had finished confessing. Macahan, as a courtesy, did not put him in irons but warned him that if he made any attempt to escape, he'd be shot. The two of them then left the office and watched by all the shocked employees, walked outside.

Across the street Melody and Liberty stood in the shade outside McGee's, arguing over the art of boiling good and bad coffee. They broke off when they saw Macahan escorting Avery to the marshal's office, and quickly crossed over and joined them.

Nearby, an impudent-looking, tow-headed boy sat in the sunbaked dirt, teasing a scorpion that was tied by string to a stick. He kept prodding it until the scorpion tried to sting him with its arched tail. Each time the boy responded by jerking the stick upward, lifting the scorpion into the air, where it hung, twisting and struggling from the end of the string.

On seeing Avery being escorted by Melody and the others to the marshal's office, the boy quickly rolled up the string, tying the now-helpless scorpion against the stick, then jumped up and ran off in the direction of the Hinkley Mansion.

It was stiflingly hot in the marshal's office and flies buzzed sluggishly against the window. Garrett sat behind his desk, feet up, hands clasped across his chest, enjoying a *siesta*.

He waked instantly as Macahan, Melody and Liberty entered with Avery and from the looks on their faces, especially Avery's, knew that he'd been sold out. His gun-belt hung over the back of the chair and as imperceptibly as he could, he inched his hand toward the holstered Colt.

'Go ahead,' Melody told him grimly.

'I'd love an excuse to kill you.'

Garrett froze, grinned like a schoolboy caught cheating, and re-clasped his hands across his chest.

''Fraid I can't give you that pleasure,' he said.

'But you *can* give me your gun and your badge,' Macahan said. He stuck his big, thick-fingered hand out, adding: '*Pronto.*'

Garrett dropped his feet from the desk and reached for his gun-belt.

Instantly Melody and Liberty tensed, ready to draw if Garrett tried to grab his Colt.

He didn't. Moving slowly, he handed Macahan the gun-belt and then his badge.

'Reckon this means we're no longer partners?' he said to Avery. He laughed, trying to hide his rage as he added: 'See you in prison, *amigo.*'

Avery paled but didn't say anything.

'Put them in separate cells,' Macahan told Melody.

Melody started toward Garrett and

then stopped as the door burst open and Regan stormed in. Behind her the tow-headed boy sat in the doorway, wide-eyed and eager to hear what was about to unfold.

Out of breath from hurrying, Regan gave Melody a withering look and then turned to Macahan.

'You're making a dreadful mistake, marshal. My father could not possibly have done anything that warrants putting him in jail!'

'I understand your feelings, Miss Avery,' Macahan said gently. 'But I suggest you save your breath and send for your father's lawyer. He's going to need him.'

'I've already sent for him,' Regan said angrily. 'And believe me, when he gets through with you, you'll wish you'd listened to me!' To her father she added: 'Don't worry, Daddy. You'll be out of here in no time.'

Avery smiled lovingly at his daughter and with more feeling than anyone would have expected, stroked her cheek for a moment before saying: 'I love you, Little Girl. Always remember that.'

'Oh, Daddy,' she began.

He stopped her. 'Go home, sweetheart — '

'But — '

'No, no, don't argue. Just go home. Please.'

Then as Regan didn't move:

'Go on, Little One. There's nothing you or anyone can do for me right now.' He turned to Liberty, saying: 'I'd appreciate it if you'd lock me in my cell.'

Liberty looked at Macahan, who nodded. She then led Avery back to the cell area.

'If you had anything to do with this,' Regan told Melody, 'I'll never forgive you.' She turned and stormed out before he could respond.

Melody wanted more than anything to go after her. But he didn't. Instead, he turned to Garrett, saying, 'Let's go,' and escorted him to his cell.

Macahan, noticing the tow-headed

boy sitting in the doorway, gave a resigned sigh and shook his head at him.

'It's times like these, sonny,' he said wearily, 'when this badge of mine gets to weighing awful heavy.'

The boy looked up at the veteran lawman. Gone was his usual impudence. In its place was a look of compassion, as if he understood the marshal's underlying pain. For several moments he didn't say anything as he searched for a way to make the lawman feel better.

Then it hit him. He'd share his only possession. Holding up his stick, he quickly he unraveled the string so that the scorpion dangled, struggling, at the end.

'Wanna see it dance?' he asked Macahan.

'Sure.'

The boy looked delighted. 'No one else can do it, you know? Not like me.'

'I bet they can't.'

'I'll show you how to do it so you

won't get stung. It's easy once you get the hang of it.'

'Most things are,' Macahan said, smiling. 'And that's the truth of it.'

We do hope that you have enjoyed reading this large print book.

Did you know that all of our titles are available for purchase?

We publish a wide range of high quality large print books including:
Romances, Mysteries, Classics
General Fiction
Non Fiction and Westerns

Special interest titles available in large print are:
The Little Oxford Dictionary
Music Book, Song Book
Hymn Book, Service Book

Also available from us courtesy of Oxford University Press:
Young Readers' Dictionary
(large print edition)
Young Readers' Thesaurus
(large print edition)

For further information or a free brochure, please contact us at:
Ulverscroft Large Print Books Ltd.,
The Green, Bradgate Road, Anstey,
Leicester, LE7 7FU, England.
Tel: (00 44) **0116 236 4325**
Fax: (00 44) **0116 234 0205**

REAPER

Lee Clinton

The Indian Territory is a hellhole of lawlessness. Deputies are gunned down in cold blood, and outlaws are trading arms to renegades. In desperation, a bold and secret plan is designed by two senior US marshals — recruit a new and unknown deputy, who can operate independently to hunt down and kill three notorious outlaws in reprisal. But has the right man been selected? Walter Garfield's background seems more than a little shady, and he appears to have his own agenda . . .